TENTH BIRTHDAY

by EVAN COMMAGER

with drawings by DON SIBLEY

THE BOBBS-MERRILL COMPANY, INC.
Publishers

INDIANAPOLIS   NEW YORK

First Edition

To H.S.C.

CONTENTS

I

Margaret Spears's
tenth birthday
April 22, 1844

Margaret Spears's

TENTH BIRTHDAY

April 22, 1844

AGGIE SPEARS waked on her tenth birthday to a sound of singing. Outside her windows every bird on Three Creeks Plantation seemed to be trying to bust its throat. Inside her room there was a mosquitery sound that resolved itself into a chant: "Happy birfday gif', happy birfday gif', two people gwine git happy birfday gif'!" And there was Dollbaby by her bed as usual, but jumping up and down this morning and giggling and gurgling as she sang. Maggie leaped from bed, grabbed Dollbaby's hands, and they pranced round and round the big room singing "Happy Birfday Gif' " till Mammy's voice pierced the noise.

"You chillun, don't you stop that ruckus, Maggie's pa'll be up there! He in the sitting room right underneath you, and he gittin' more 'n tired of your big foots bamming over he head."

The girls stopped at once—children didn't makes ruckuses round Maggie's pa. But why wasn't he in his office like he belonged to be till breakfasttime? Dollbaby put both her hands over all the lower part of her face. Above them her eyes danced at Maggie, and little bursts of giggles kept sprouting out of them. Maggie attacked the pile of clothes Dollbaby had laid out for her, and was dressed in no time—even her petticoats and pantalets seemed to know it was her birthday; they rustled starchily like singing. She sloshed some water in the washbowl, transferred a few drops of it to her face, then rubbed hard with a towel.

Starting to brush her hair, she looked at Dollbaby's. "Why I declare, Dollbaby, your hair is unwropped."

"Sho is. This our big day, enny?"

Maggie secretly thought Dollbaby looked nicer with all the little string-wrapped clumps of hair standing merrily up as usual than she did with a great bush of it making her face look smaller, but she wouldn't say so for worlds. Anyhow, it was delicious to be different on your birthday, every way you could. So she gave her own hair at least ten extra licks to match Dollbaby's efforts, then snatched up two pink camellias from the bowl of them she had brought up to her room yesterday and stuck one in Dollbaby's hair and one in her own.

"Now we look like a birthday, and we better hit the grit downstairs so I don't be late for breakfast."

She grabbed Dollbaby's hand, and they ran through the wide hall and down the staircase with a soft scuffling of bare feet.

Mamma and Pa were just sitting down to the breakfast table when the little girls walked sedately in. Mamma beamed at them and called, "Happy birthday, little girls!" but Pa waited till Maggie had sat down and unfolded her napkin, her back straight and one inch from the back of her chair, and Dollbaby had taken her stand behind the chair, before he laid down the Charleston *Mercury* and addressed them:

"Margaret, I wish you a happy birthday. Dollbaby, I wish you a happy birthday."

"Thank you, suh," chorused the girls, Dollbaby bobbing so convulsively that her knee cracked against Maggie's chair and would have precipitated an attack of giggles if Unc' Anson, handing the hominy around, hadn't given them a quelling look. Unc' Anson put a heap of mind on keeping the two girls what he called mannerable—too much

13

mind, Maggie often thought. Still, she believed even if she could have her rathers, she wouldn't really want Unc' Anson any different. He was so stately that just to be rebuked by him somehow showed you were somebody. Pa was impressive, so fine and big and tight in his clothes; she thought he probably looked like the Squire in *Bracebridge Hall* (*dear* Mr. Irving, to make you know more what your own people were like, through his); but Unc' Anson, so tall

14

and straight and white-haired, looked like a king. And it was pride in his white folks that made him so strict with her; he probably thought she was in danger of being spoiled because she was the only child left at home now that her older brother was in the west and her older sisters were married and Edwin was down there at the Citadel in Charleston— there was a two-child gap between her and Ed because of the typhoid in 1834, just before she was born.

She smiled up at Unc' Anson as she took a dolloping spoonful of hominy, and he smiled back indulgently. "I gives you Happy Birthday too, little missie. And you better have more butter on your homly. Hit'll stren'then you for your birthday frolicking."

"And what frolicking you can do!" exclaimed Mamma. "Your father says that you need not go for your lessons today."

What bliss! Maggie had been dreading lessons today. She had worked yesterday till her slate was almost worn through with rubbing out about three tierces of sugar on a hideous problem involving the rule of three, and had not solved it. Now maybe she would have a chance to get it done before tomorrow. Then the other children from the plantations near by who had lessons with the Rev'en', as Dollbaby called him, wouldn't have a chance to laugh at her as they so often did during arithmetic—not during reading or Webster's blue-back speller, though. Maybe, even, Pa would help her with it if she took her slate along when she went to his office to read Josephus to him at five as always. That would be good. It would mean she not only got the problem done, but would have less time to read Josephus, who she wished every day (except Saturday which was rations day with Pa at the commissary) had never been born. She suspected Mamma sympathized with her about Josephus. Mamma was frivolous. Probably because of having some French blood, the connection all said. They all loved her for it, and Maggie thought Pa probably liked it pretty much too, because she overheard Mamma say to him once in her most frivolous voice, "James, you stern old Roman," and you could hear a smile in Pa's voice as he said back, "Deborah, you incorrigible little flibbertigibbet!"

He didn't really think that, though, because Maggie once heard him tell the Rev'en' that the mistress of a plantation worked harder than anybody else on it. And he was mighty proud because Mamma always took such good care of their people that there was almost never any sickness in the Quar-

16

ters she couldn't tend to by herself, with Dr. Gunn's book. And she was the one who made it a happy plantation too, Pa said.

Maggie was so busy eating battycakes and thinking about Josephus and the French and such things her father had to rustle his newspaper at her before she realized he had said "Daughter!"

"Yessir?"

"I rode by the Reverend Mr. Entwhistle's yesterday evening and informed him that though I was opposed to anything interfering with education, even the education of a young female, I thought your work since Christmas was of sufficient merit to warrant your being given a holiday."

"Oh, Pa, thank you," said Maggie with a slight blush for those tierces of sugar.

"Furthermore, it will be my pleasure to excuse you from our daily reading of Josephus this evening so you and Dollbaby can play all day till sundown."

"Oh, Pa!" said Maggie rapturously. Then all of a sudden she showed she was really older today by lowering her voice and quenching her smile and saying demurely, "That will be nice, sir," because, after all, Pa really liked Josephus. Tactful, she was being, as befitted ten years old.

"Very good."

Mamma, who had been reading her mail, now looked up to smile in her eye-crinkling way at Maggie and Dollbaby. "Dollbaby," she said, "did you have an extra good breakfast this morning?"

"Yes, ma'am, I sho did, ma'am. I had bacon, not just whiteside, and 'bout a gallon of buttermilk."

"But you didn't have battercakes. Go out to the kitchen and tell Ailcy to give you some, with plenty of molasses."

"Yes, *ma'am*." Dollbaby started to dance out, then remembered her ten years and Marse James, and disappeared in a dignified strut.

"Dear little Dollbaby!" said Mamma. "That was a good idea to make her birthday the same as Maggie's."

"Very clever, Deborah," said Pa. He meant it was kind and thoughtful—not what some people mean by clever.

Dollbaby hadn't been born on Three Creeks Plantation. She and Reba, her mother, had come from Judge Miles's place about six years ago because Joab, Pa's coachman, wanted to marry Reba, whose first husband was dead. Maggie and Dollbaby had been inseparable from the first day they saw each other, and were the same age, so Mamma, when she found out Reba didn't rightly know just when Dollbaby's birthday fell, suggested that the two little girls have the same birthday. Reba was pretty sure Dollbaby had been born in the same month as Maggie; she rickollected her first husband had fotched her a bunch of yellow jessamines while she was lying in bed with the baby, and she could remember to this day how pretty they smelled. So it seemed to Mamma the practical thing to have the birthdays together, and to Maggie and Dollbaby it seemed the grandest thing imaginable to be twins. Next to Mamma and Pa and Edwin, Maggie loved Dollbaby best in the world, which of course so far was just Three Creeks Plantation, and I am afraid Dollbaby loved Maggie best of anybody anywhere. Her ma wasn't frivolous and soft like Maggie's mother; Reba was such a sanctified woman that she was ready to larrup Dollbaby for 'most anything.

"I sent Dollbaby to the kitchen, Maggie," said Mamma, "because we have a present for you she wouldn't like, but it might make her feel left out to give it to you with her here."

She pulled a package from under her chair. Maggie seized it eagerly; she could tell from its shape it was a book. Last year, in exactly the same ceremony, she had been given *Pilgrim's Progress*. Nothing so exciting as a book; 'most anything else could be raised or made on the place, like a new dress or hat or shoes, but a book had to come from far off.

It was called *The Ingoldsby Legends or Mirth and Marvels*. It had lovely drawings.

Pa was flapping his newspaper again. "My factor in Charleston got this for you, all the way from England," he announced. "I must say, though, that the subtitle, *Mirth and Marvels,* makes me very uncertain whether you should have it. I fear modern children think too much about mirth."

"Oh, Pa, I'm sure—I'm sure it's a very *improving* book," gasped Maggie. She had just caught sight of the lines:

> There's a horrid old hag in a steeple-crown'd hat,
> Round her neck they have tied to a hempen cravat
> A Dead Man's hand and a dead Tom Cat!

"Please could I go read in it a little while?"

"Toreckly. Finish your victuals first," said Pa, who was only halfway through his.

"Don't you want another battercake,

dear?" asked Mamma, swinging one temptingly from her fork.

"Oh, please, ma'am, I've done et all the battycakes I can hold," said Maggie, clutching the book tightly.

"Margaret!" said her father, and his lips folded together for a second, the way they always did when he was plumb exasperated. "Margaret," he repeated, "you are now ten years old. Don't you consider it is high time for you to start talking like a lady? I have told you children over and over that I wish you to imitate your colored people in manners and good humor, but *not* in speech. 'Done et!' I am astonished."

"Oh, Pa, I am sorry," Maggie cried. "I mean, I have had an elegant sufficiency, thank you."

Pa's heavy face almost succumbed to a smile. "Very well," he said. "You may go."

Then as Maggie was pushing her chair back, he looked at her again, and this time his face gave into the smile. "Daughter," he said, "since this is your tenth birthday, I shall take the risk of your being puffed-up and tell you that as I look at you on this occasion, I am minded to say to you something I read last night in a better book than that one. The lines are

21

'In thy face I see
The map of honour, truth and loyalty.' "

Maggie was overwhelmed. Outspoken praise from Pa! The words were probably from one of those Shakespeare books, as they were mostly what he read, outside of the Charleston *Mercury* and the *Congressional Globe* and that old Josephus. And what heavenly words to have put to oneself! She was practically trembling with pleasure and embarrassment.

Mother came to her rescue. "What *I* think about your face on your tenth birthday, Maggie," she said, "is that it's mighty pretty!"

She gave a sassy look at Pa, and followed Maggie out of the dining room. "Go get Dollbaby and come up to my room," she directed.

Maggie sped out to the kitchen house, stumping her toe in her haste, but it hardly even bled and didn't hurt a bit.

"C'mon, Dob, Mamma wants us."

Dollbaby sprang up, wiped considerable molasses off her face with the back of her hand, and ran with Maggie back into the Big House and up the stairs.

Mamma was standing in her room chuckling with pleasure and holding in her arms two dolls.

And what dolls! Maggie and Dollbaby had large families of corncob and rag dolls, but the like of these two dolls had never been seen or imagined by either of them—probably not by anybody. China heads, with beautiful black hair and brown eyes painted on one, and beautiful yellow hair and blue eyes painted on the other, and smiles like angels' own painted on both. And china hands and feet, the feet painted with neat little boots and white stockings. And the brown-eyed doll had on a costume— you couldn't call it just a dress—made of the same

indigo-dyed cloth as Maggie's Sunday dress, and the blue-eyed one's costume was of the sweet-gum-dyed cloth of Dollbaby's Sunday dress. Both costumes were made grown-up, though, not little-girl. And the pantalets and petticoats were even finer than Maggie's Sunday ones. And when Maggie and Dollbaby drew breath from mirating over these things, Mamma pointed out on her bed two piles of other costumes, all colors and all equally fashionable—that is to say, more fashionable than any real young ladies' clothes the girls had ever seen, and most of Maggie's young-lady cousins were very fashionable indeed, being given to St. Cecilia balls and the like.

"They are in the latest style, copied from Mrs. Breeden's last *Ladies' Book*," said Mamma complacently.

"Oh, Mamma, they look even stylisher than Cousin Sue!" declared Maggie.

"I 'clare, they mos' as pretty as you is, Miss Deborah," said Dollbaby, showing her raising.

"Well now, youall run out to the sewing room and thank Aunt Dilly. She made every one of these clothes herself. I reckon the good Lord musta sent all that rain last week so's the fieldwomen could come in and help her with the ordinary sewing."

The little girls flew away to the sewing room, and there had a very satisfactory time with

Aunt Dilly, who pointed out every refinement in all the costumes to them and to Janie Lame and Kizzie and Aunt Sally and Mom Liza, who left their shirts and pants making to cluster around. All very exciting. But after 'most an hour of all this chatter, Maggie began to feel bored and very conscious of the book under her arm.

She had a bright idea. "Dob, you ain't put out your baid yit—I mean," she said, thinking of her father, "you haven't aired your matt'ess yet. You better run down to the Quarters and do that," she said in a moral tone.

"I sho-lawd better," replied Dollbaby, equally moral.

"And when you git back, we'll hitch up Unca Sam's billy goat and make him ride us, or sump'n else fun."

Dollbaby's eyes gleamed. She swooped up her doll, by then filially named Debo-reba, and scampered off.

"You better go find your ma and show her Debo-reba whilst you there," Maggie called after her.

Then she picked up her doll, now Angelica, said good-bys to the sewing women, putting on all the manners she could, and went off to find a place where she could get into those *Ingoldsby Leg-*

ends or Mirth and Marvels again. Now she didn't plan to go hide; somehow her feet just naturally took her onto the path to the spring. The one 'way off through the pine wood whose waters were medicinal, Pa said, so nobody was apt to come there and interrupt her. That wasn't very nice of her to go where Dollbaby couldn't find her on their birthday,

26

but she didn't really aim to stay there much time at all. She would just look through this book a little bit. Pa would *want* her to be interested in it. So she struck off down the path in a sort of guilty lope.

Usually when she was going down that path, she would stop when she came to the burying ground, off to one side of it just before you got to the pine woods, and look at her great-grandmother's grave, maybe put a flower on it, even. She liked to think of her great-grandmother, Lydia Spears, how she had been a noted beauty even in Virginia, and how she had come with Great-grandfather Nathaniel into Marlboro County and had all that hard work and tribulations of making a plantation in a new country (just like in the song—"Ain't them hard trials, gre't tribulations"). And about twenty-five years afterward, along came the Revolution, with all

those hateful Tories making more trouble for Lydia and everybody.

The Revolution was exciting, though; Maggie would have lived during it if she'd had her rathers. That nice Thomas boy over at Blenheim had told her tales about how his great-uncle Major Tristram Thomas had scared off the British and taken lots of them prisoners by putting up make-believe guns out of logs right down there at Hunt's Bluff where the boats from her father's factor in Charleston unloaded, and Maggie was sure she could have helped somebody do something like that if she had lived then.

She liked to stop in the burying ground and think about those things. Today, though, she didn't give a thought to her grandmother's grave, at least not more than the smallest possible "respectful thought"; she managed that because Pa said she must always pause for respectful thought when she passed her forebears' graves. She hurried past into the pine woods, hugging her book. In a minute she was sitting on a bench in the little house Pa had had built over the spring in the hope that it would attract people there to drink the medicinal water.

She fell into a sort of spell, and for the next three hours nothing existed for her except places like Tapton Everard and Shurland Castle and people like the Honourable Augustus Sucklethumbkin and Father Fothergill and Mrs. Botherby—certainly not poor little Dollbaby.

When she came out of the spell, one foot had gone to sleep, her head was humming with a sort of drunkenness like when you swing too long and high, her stomach felt as if breakfast was a long time ago, and Angelica looked forlorn and forgotten lying on the bench in all her finery.

"I be june!" she exclaimed, jumping up and then hopping around on her still-awake foot. "It feels like dinnertime a'ready. Pa will say I've failed in self-control again, or sump'n like that," she told herself.

She flew up the path through the pine wood past the burying ground without the least flicker of respectful thought, through the indigo patch and the flower garden, and burst into the Big House panting, with Angelica hanging almost upside down and the guilty book held behind her draggled skirt. Mamma was in the parlor rearranging a churn full of peach-blossom branches and looking pink and pleased.

"Maggie, where *have* you been?" she exclaimed. "Dollbaby has been hunting and hunting for you all morning, and finally she went back to the Quarters looking so sad and mad. But don't stop to talk now. Run quick-like-a-rabbit upstairs and change out of that dress into something clean and pretty and brush your hair. Jeems just came running into the house and said he saw two carriages turn into the avenue and he's pretty sure it's the Bruton Forks carriages. So we'll have company for dinner, and I want you to look nice like a tenth-birthday girl. They'll be here in no time."

Then she turned to Mammy's daughter Vi'let, who was so neat and clean she had lately been changed to housemaid and who now stood poised for action in the doorway. "Did Jeems tell you the Bruton Forks carriages are coming up the avenue and we'll have company for dinner?"

"Yas'm, he done tole ev'ybody."

"Now, Vi'let, you go straight to Ailcy, and tell her I said to make about six times as many biscuits as usual because she knows what Mr. McQueen is with biscuits, and make riz corn bread—now don't let her tell you the master likes corn pone better; I know he does but riz corn bread is nicer for company—and serve cheese straws with the soup instead of light bread, and use my dishes from England on the table, and tell Unc' Anson be sure he has on a coat that's nice and stiff-starched, and to fetch up some peach brandy and to slice the ham as thin as paper—Mrs. McQueen is the best ham slicer in the county and we must show her what we can do—and if there aren't enough chickens already picked in the cold room, Jeems will have to catch some more and pick 'em quick but tell him be more than careful about the tiny feathers—I hope he won't have to because catching chickens just before dinner is a trifling way to do, isn't it?—and tell Ailcy remember Mr. McQueen eats as much rice as the master does himself and don't let it run out like last time. And tell her—and *this* is what you must remember—tell her I say flavor all the vegetables just the way I've been telling her. Remind her all these people expect mighty fancy cooking from her because my great-grandmother was French. Now run, Vi'let."

Vi'let ran, tittering with expectation, because there would be company in the kitchen too. Maybe Old Willett and Young Willett would be driving the Bruton Forks carriages, and Young Willett was the man who held onto the flaming kerosene ball longest at the last Saturday-night frolic at Blenheim. She and the other house servants loved these times when they all of a sudden had to put a dozen extra names in the pot, and had to run all over the place getting in fresh meat and liver pudding and sausage and such and churning ice cream and putting extra polish on the silver. Things got kinder dull in the Big House with all the young'uns except Maggie gone, and it was good when a passel of company turned up.

Mrs. Spears put the last peach branch back into place, pushed the churn holding them back into the fireplace, and called somebody to wipe up the water she had spilled. Then she looked earnestly at her pretty face in the gilt mirror, twisted a curl into place, picked up her skirts, luckily of her second-best dress because of Maggie's birthday, and skipped out to the front piazza, where she stood laughing with joy when the Bruton Forks carriages rolled up.

Then there was commotion aplenty. Miss Sally McQueen and her husband and Miss Sally's mother and Miss Sally's sister-in-law, Miss Mary Grace Matthews, and her husband, who were visiting Miss Sally, were all laughing and talking on the front piazza when Maggie came down in her pink dress. And best of all, there was Cousin Sue Grayson herself, stylisher than ever, and gladder to see Maggie than anybody else. That's because Sue loved to tell about the balls and barbecues she went to, and Maggie was the best possible listener.

"You know why we came today, Deborah?" said sweet fat Miss Sally McQueen. "It's because I remembered it was Maggie's birthday, so we all just piled into the carriages and came rushing over to say Happy Birthday."

"Got here in less than an hour," said Mr. McQueen, looking proudly at his horses as they were being led away.

"This is very clever of you, very clever, indeed," said Pa. "I suggest that we all go into the parlor and drink a health to Margaret while we wait for our dinner."

So that's what they did. Maggie felt very proud when she saw all the glasses of blackberry wine lifted in her honor.

Mamma was such a good housekeeper that dinner was served at two o'clock sharp as usual. When you went to some houses unexpectedly, as at the Flats where Mr. Conroy had a Philadelphia wife, dinner might get thrown back an hour or more, but nothing like that ever happened at Three Creeks Plantation with Mamma. A good thing too: nothing aggravated Pa like inefficiency, inside the house or out in the fields.

Anyhow, dinner was mighty good as well as on time, and Maggie felt sodden with food when the end of all the eating and talking had come. She felt sleepy too, maybe because Mr. Joe Matthews had given her a taste of his peach brandy. She did plan to go find Dollbaby, but it wasn't going to be any fun to go walking down to the Quarters, sleepy as she felt.

Her conscience was sleepy too. It didn't even stir when Cousin Sue said, "How 'bout for you and me to go lie down in your room awhile? I'm plumb worn out from that dance last night. I'll tell you all about it, and you can brush my hair if you want." She eagerly agreed, pushing Dollbaby right out of her mind, and pretty soon she and Cousin Sue, stripped to three petticoats, were lying on the big bed in her cool room with the blinds drawn, and Cousin Sue was telling her things about the dance. All the things she told seemed to start with "He said" and after a long while Maggie got a little bored. She didn't think much of any he's she had seen yet.

Finally she broke in. "Cousin Sue, did you ever read the *Ingoldsby Legends?*"

"A book, you mean, honey? Law, honey, I don't care so much for books. I'd rather just read letters, honey. Did I ever tell you about that letter

34

with poetry in it I got from the nice boy in Alabama? You know——"

"Yeah, I remember," said Maggie, and yawned.

Cousin Sue yawned too, and in just a minute there she was fast asleep, curled up like a kitten with her curly hair well brushed by Maggie spread out over the pillow. Maggie looked at her affectionately; it wasn't against anybody if they didn't like the same things you liked; kin is kin.

She decided she would go to sleep herself. But, it turned out, something wouldn't let her. Squeeze her eyes tight shut as she would, try as she would to make pictures come in them as pictures came every night when she shut them tight, do everything she knew to make sleep come, sleep still wouldn't come. So she opened her eyes and faced it—there was something that was wrong and she wasn't ever going to be able to sleep till she had done something about it. She sighed drearily, so vigorously that Sue's long eyelashes stirred. Maggie froze into stillness; she didn't want any more talk right now—anyhow not about beaux from Alabama and such.

What did she want? Well, she reckoned she wanted to get back to feeling the way she had early this morning. She smiled as she remembered

Mamma holding the dolls so proudly, and she smiled more deeply as she remembered Pa saying,

> "In thy face I see
> The map of honour, truth and loyalty."

Then the smile vanished. *There* was the trouble! Pa believed those words when he said them, and she really believed them too about herself when he said them. Because she knew she did try hard for honor, truth and loyalty; she knew she really thought more of those things than she did of the things the Sunday-school people wanted you to have —maybe she favored Pa that way, because in spite of all Mamma or the neighbors could say, he would *not* go to any church though he was all the time reading about religions like in Josephus; oh dear, didn't she feel bad enough without that old Josephus popping up in her mind? She went back to her relentless search for why she couldn't sleep. It was because she had agreed in her mind with Pa that she had honor, truth and loyalty—but not being conceited about it really; she knew there wasn't much credit to her in having them, because there wasn't anything in the life at Three Creeks to keep her from them, with everybody in the house and in the Quarters so

36

kind-loving and actually helping her every minute of the day to be good. And now, just after having
the lovely words she valued most applied to her by
none other than her father, she was having to admit
they didn't fit her at all. Her father had been wrong
about her, and she had been wrong about herself.
She had no loyalty. Anybody who could treat her
best friend the way she had treated Dollbaby today
had no loyalty—probably no truth and honor either,
as she couldn't imagine losing one of the three without losing the others.

No wonder she couldn't sleep, she
thought dramatically.

She swung her feet over the side of the
bed and slid quietly down to the floor, put on her
dress silently and crept downstairs. First, she thought
she would go to Mamma and make full confession;
then she knew she would go where the real help was,
even if the help would hurt. Maybe Pa would switch
her?

She crept out the back door since she
heard the McQueens and the Matthewses and her
Mamma talking, more gently now, musingly even,
on the front piazza. She made her way out to the
office and walked in the open door. Pa was there at
his desk; he didn't let company keep him away from

his business, the way most men did. There was Zack
too, in from the field this time of day.

Her father looked up. "Come in, Mag-
gie. You must wait a moment. Zack came first and
he hasn't told me what he wants yet. Go ahead,
Zack."

Zack was twisting his cornhusk hat nervously. "Well, suh, I done thought I better tell you,
suh, 'cause I knows how you feel about your people
and ain't gwine allow no projecking with them or
'busing of 'em."

"That's right. So kindly get on with
your story."

"Well, suh, Marse James, Jupiter done
come home from Hunt's Bluff with his face cut open.
Moughta put his eyes out 'cept the good Lord take
care of him."

"How did it happen?" Pa's lips sho were
folded together.

"Well, suh, Marse James, seem like he
were driving the wagon home from Hunt's Bluff and
just as he git right in front of the big gate at Marse
Jimpson's place, Marse Jimpson come riding out on
he horse so fast that when he horse see the wagon
right in front of him he have to rear up, and Marse
Jimpson have a hard time staying on, it so sudden.

I reckon Jupiter mought have grin—Marse Jimpson musta look mighty funny having to work to stay on a horse and him the best rider in the county. Anyhow Mr. Jimpson holler 'You impident nigger' and slash him cross the face with he crop."

"I see. You can go. Tell Joab to come round with my horse right away."

"Oh, Pa," Maggie exclaimed, "you won't go see old Jimpson, will you? He totes a gun—everybody says so—and he drinks."

"That will be my concern, Margaret, not yours. And children do not speak of grown-folks' failings. Now why have you come?"

He settled down and looked at her as if he really wanted to know.

Then it all came pouring out.

"Pa, I thought I better come tell you. You may oughter whup me. I been really bad this time."

"Have you hurt anyone or told a lie?"

"No, suh. But in a way I did worse. After you said that about honor, truth and loyalty, I went off and be'd as disloyal as anybody could be. Because it was disloyal to Dollbaby. And I bet she is crying and hollering right now."

"Tell me what you have done."

So Maggie told it all, how the book tempted her and she did fall; how Cousin Sue and the beaux had tempted her and she did fall some more.

Before she finished, she was almost enjoying herself; low-rating oneself is actually a kind of luxurious feeling, she found, and it was exhilarating to have all Pa's attention this way. He sat quite still, hand in front of his mouth and a finger stroking his cheek reflectively.

When she ended with "Now I feel like a hound-dog," he stared at her a moment, then took his hand down and said, "You should. Disloyalty to a friend, especially a dependent friend, is contemptible. It's a thing that lots of us fall into, though, without meaning to. The practical thing to do is to leave off repining, go find Dollbaby, and make the rest of her day so happy that she will forget this morning. Don't be too apologetic. In other words, don't dramatize. That's a good thing to learn early—don't dramatize yourself, not even your mistakes. Do you know what dramatize means?"

Maggie gazed into his calm blue eyes and felt a brand-new surge of affection for this old rock of a father. "I believe I do, Pa," she said. "I believe maybe I kinder do it a lot. Maybe I'll stop, though, now I'm ten."

"I expect you will have all the grown-up virtues now you are ten," Pa said, and suddenly he was grinning widely at her—he felt as near as Mamma always did.

"Please, Pa, when I've played with Dollbaby awhile, can I come back and read Josephus? I'd . . . I'd like to."

"No, no. Stay with Dollbaby till her supper bell. You will be as happy as ever because she

41

will forgive the book for coming between you, though she may be somewhat wroth at first. And being a sensible little girl, or rather a sensible ten-year-old girl, you will appreciate Dollbaby just the same even after you begin having other interests. She knows that because she is sensible and ten years old too. And she will later on have other interests too, you know. She probably has talents you haven't got."

"Oh, Pa, she has! She can cook. And she can make heap prettier things out of clay. And she learns me—I mean she teaches me—better things than I teach her. I taught her not to be scared of hants, but she taught me not to be scared of mules. And . . . and if she could read Josephus, she would read him heaps better than I do. She has a very patient character," said Maggie, triumphantly knowing that her elegant words would bring a flicker to her father's face.

They did, but he said merely, "Run along now. I hear Joab with my horse."

Maggie ran along to the Quarters, where she found Dollbaby swinging her legs from the little porch on her cabin, looking downcast but not sullen as Maggie feared, because she was holding Debo-reba in her lap and it was hard for Dollbaby to be ill-humored any time, and just plain impossible with

42

Debo-reba in her arms. So she greeted Maggie with no recriminations, accepted the broken cheese straw from Maggie's pocket affably, and even explained that she woulda been behind Maggie's chair to holp her with her dinner but Unc' Anson say better not with all them companies there.

So peace and something more were established, and they got in a heap of playing before sundown. A little too much maybe. They tried hitching up Unca Sam's billy goat, but agreed they were bored with that after he butted a big tear in Maggie's pink dress. Then Maggie went to fetch Angelica, and they decided to baptize the dolls—the

Episcopal way though, because no matter how religious you were, you couldn't totally immerse those costumes. So they took them down to the medicinal spring and solemnly baptized them, and Dollbaby claimed she could rest her head easier when night came, now her child had salvation. Then they each had a drink of medicinal water out of the long-handled gourds hanging in the springhouse. Then they wondered if anybody could dip water out of the spring quick as it came in. So they tried to see. And when Pa got home from the Jimpson Place, leaving a good piece of his mind behind him, they were throwing water all over the springhouse, dipping it out so fast and making such a whooping and hollering that he came to the spring to find out was it a rattlesnake maybe. When he saw what was happening and them both soaked to the skin and yelling like Indians, he just stood there and looked at them. As for them, they just picked up their dolls and tore past him, lickety-split up the path. They both knew perfectly they would have got a switching, hadn't it been their birthday.

But it *was* their birthday.

II

Nellie Spears Thomas'
tenth birthday

September 7, 1864

Nellie Spears Thomas'

TENTH BIRTHDAY

September 7, 1864

"This war will last forever, it seems.
Our Mother's eyes have lost their dreams,
But her spirit in them always beams,
    And she does never weep.
She knows our Southern cause is right,
And that Lee and Father will win the fight,
And that some day our family will reunite. . . ."

NELLIE chewed her pencil while she ran over
rhymes for weep. "Then for joy we'll leap."
. . . "Then we'll eat a heap." . . . "The
Yankees their punishment will reap." Then she had
a practical idea, crossed out "weep" and substituted
"cry," wrote in for the last line, "In God's own by-
and-by," and leaned back, warm with satisfaction.
That last line was not only poetic but pious, down-

right hymnal. What an achievement, considering they hadn't been able to go to church since last February when the last horse, old May-Day, died and Mother said they couldn't use either of the mules to go into town on Sunday because the poor old mules that were left had to work so hard all week trying to make a crop.

Nellie copied the poem in her fairest hand, sadly altered, she feared, by her months away from school. Mother gave her lessons of course every day she had time, but maybe was too tired to be strict about penmanship as Miss Breeden at the Academy

48

used to be. At the top of the page she wrote "Nellie Thomas, Sept. 7, 1864 (her Tenth Birthday)." Then she thought, Suppose Mother doesn't remember this is my birthday. It will upset her to think that things are bad enough to make her forget her child's birthday. And this poem was supposed to cheer her.

So she carefully erased the "(her Tenth Birthday)." Then she thought some more. Then she tore up the poem. And that was pain for Nellie, because she thought well of everything she wrote, probably because Father did—he used to read everything she wrote, little poems about cotton picking, little paragraphs about how the acres of grapevines looked from underneath, and such, and he would look stern and impartial and then say, "You are, by gift of God, able to write."

So it wounded her to tear up this poem, but she wished to be enough like Father to do anything that would keep sadness or discomfort away from Mother.

Having tossed the bits of paper into the fireplace to await the first fire of the coming winter (for Nellie was not much of a housekeeper; that was one of the things that led her to believe she must be going to be Literary), she went downstairs, carefully looking as if this were an ordinary day. But at the foot of the stairs, her mother was standing, looking as if this were a very special day indeed.

"Happy birthday, Nellie dear!"

Nellie looked from her smiling face to the disapproving one of the hall clock as it started to strike in a censorious fashion. "Goodness, Mother, it's nine o'clock, and I've been *dawdling* upstairs!"

"I know. I wanted you to sleep late, to make the day different. And I have a present for you!"

And there on the horsehair sofa that Father had given Mother just a month before the War started and he went away with all the Marlboro County young men at his heels (so Mrs. Judge Patterson said), lay a dress. What a dress! (Nellie's mind flew to the goose in Mr. Dickens' *Christmas Carol*.) It was black calico of course; that was about the only kind of cloth they were able to get from England; Father had chuckled, but maybe sadly, when he brought it home on that wonderful furlough last winter, and said, "The English know—they've had lots of wars—they know black cloth is what the ladies will need. And between their good will and our blockade-runners, here is some cloth for you, Maggie."

But with this dress, you wouldn't know it was made of black cloth for wives or mothers or sweethearts or sisters of people who were killed in the War, which is to say for almost any female in the South; this dress was dazzling with yards and yards of white braid going in undulating rows up and down the skirt, up and down the bodice, up and down the beautiful sleeves. It was the gayest dress Nellie had ever seen, and she could remember dresses from before the war.

"Oh, Mother!" she gasped. "But oh, Mother, Father meant you to have a dress from that cloth."

"He'd rather you, Nellie," said Mother. "I can always have dresses, and will after the War is over, but you won't ever have a tenth birthday again."

"But where did the beautiful white trimming come from? It's beautifuler than—beautifuler than Father in his uniform!"

"Oh, it's just one of the sheets. I could easily spare it," said Mother airily.

Nellie said no more, and forced her eyes to keep from filling with tears. She knew that all the sheets, except two each for every member of the family left at home, had gone as bandages to the army, and she knew that her mother, raised so delicately on Grandfather's plantation with its hundred slaves, was proposing to sleep henceforward with one sheet —underneath or on top? she wondered ridiculously.

"And I have a cup of almost-coffee for your breakfast! No parched peanuts or okra about it!"

"Oh, Mother, no! I couldn't. You've been saving it for Father's next furlough." But how wonderful, Nellie thought, to have her birthday so important to Mother!

"He'd like you to have it for a birthday treat, even though you are too young to drink coffee—and that will make it taste even better. Besides, Father won't have another furlough any time soon, the way things are going. They can't spare people like him for a minute, not even to come home and get the crop in."

But Mother kept her voice just proud, not worried. She put a big spoonful of molasses into the steaming coffee, handed it to Nellie, and then sat down across the table and folded her hands in a tea-party sort of way—just to show what a great day it was, because Nellie knew Mother had a thousand things to do and would be working even later to-night because of sitting down now. She smiled lovingly over the coffee cup while her mother chattered. Then Aunt Dozy shuffled in bringing Nellie's piece of corn bread, still good and hot and with molasses poured recklessly over it. She was giggling in the dreadful way that showed her blue gums with just the two stumps sticking in them and shrilling, "Happy birthday, little missie, you pretty as a picture," and "Gawd bless you, little missie! Gawd save you and sanctify you!"

Nellie felt her flesh crawl as it always did when Aunt Dozy got excited and pushed her wizened little black face in hers and practically danced up and down. Then her conscience smote her for letting her flesh crawl, when she knew she ought to be just thankful for Aunt Dozy. Because if Aunt Dozy and Unc' Alec hadn't stayed on when their other colored people all ran away, Mother would have to tend to everything on the place, the house and the cooking and the washing and the garden and the chickens and the cow and the cotton patch, all by herself with only Nellie to help since Martha and Bet and Maggie and Little William were all too little to do anything much except mind the baby or rock him to sleep in his cradle. Naturally the family had never had many servants, since Father was a preacher, but there had been a cook and a housemaid and some field hands, one of whom could be a coachman.

Aunt Dozy and Unc' Alec had been just sorter living on the place and doing nothing since they had grown so old, but after the War came and the others ran away, they both started working again, not so hard as Mother of course and maybe not even so hard as Nellie, but they worked, and all of a sudden got much younger-looking and sprier. Nellie supposed it was because they felt important and needed now. She wondered wryly once in a while, should they keep getting younger and younger from feeling proud, if they mightn't some day feel young enough to run away and join the Yankees, like the others. But her mother declared that Aunt Dozy and Unc' Alec stayed behind out of affection as well as from old age and a suspicion that the Yankees wouldn't really give them chitlins and white corn bread every day, like the story went.

So Nellie tried to be affectionate back to them—and she did love Unc' Alec, whom she didn't see so often, as he stayed outdoors puttering in the cotton patch or vegetables or, more often, lying asleep under the grapevine. But when he was awake and not feeling cross about his chickens getting into his vegetables, or something like that, he would sometimes tell Nellie and the other children long stories. Mostly they were about his religious experiences, probably in deference to their being preacher's children, but his religious experiences were pretty exciting. And Nellie liked to look at *his* face; it was like a gentle, puzzled monkey's, and he never yelled or stomped with laughter the way Aunt Dozy did, so you never knew if he had horrible stumps in his mouth like her.

Nellie loathed ugliness with the same shrinking that she had for snakes; that was why the War was almost as bad for her in little ways as in the big ones. She wondered sadly if she didn't really feel as keenly about the flower garden perishing from neglect and from the ugly squawking chickens they had to raise, or about her mother's hands being all red and swollen, as she did about the Ramsey twins, for instance. They had both been killed in the same battle last month. She didn't know them very well, being eight years younger, but they were Mother's second cousin's sons and the last of that name, Mother said, since of course they hadn't had time to get married before the War came. Nellie thought she ought to be thinking more of a kinswoman's sorrow (lovely phrase) and the general sadness of a name's dying out, or being killed out, than of her own angry impatience with the ugliness of daily life, all work and no play and, worst of all for her, no learning. She wanted books and learning more than anything else in the world, more than goodness even, she admitted to herself in horror. Nellie always told the truth to herself. Father had told her once that oneself was the hardest person in the world to be always and entirely truthful to, and Nellie liked to do hard things.

As she was brooding, now the delicious coffee was gone, on her unlikable qualities and even making birthday resolutions to change them by strenuous efforts at thinking more about other people besides just Father and Mother whom it was easy—oh, pleasant really—to think of first, the dining-room door opened, and Unc' Alec stood there looking piteous, like a monkey whose nut has been snatched away.

"Miss M-Margaret," he stammered, making pleading movements toward Mother, "Miss Margaret, that yaller dog done been again. He taken two more of our chickens. He taken our ole dominicker hen. She feathers scattered all over the yard. And now he commencing to come in the pure daytime. I *see* him running lickety-split with our rooster in he mouth."

The old man was almost weeping with rage. And suddenly Nellie heard a strange sound, something she hadn't heard in the whole course of the War, not even when the news came about Uncle Edwin—a great sob from her mother.

"It's too much," Mother wept. "It's too much. Those chickens are our only hope of earning a little money. What will become of my children?"

She put her head on the table and made sounds of grief and rage that froze Nellie to her chair. That was just for a moment though; then Mother raised her head and wiped her eyes. "That was wicked of me," she said painfully. "I would hate

57

for your father to know I could be so uncontrolled."

She drew a deep breath and went on, "We have been very fortunate people. We are managing to live and your dear father is still unharmed. We should be very thankful. And I ask your pardon, Nellie, for behaving in such a way. It was really just temper and not befitting a lady. And I ask your pardon, Unc' Alec."

Nellie could say nothing, but Unc' Alec made soothing motions with his shaking old hands and said, "There, Miss Margaret, don't you fret yourself! If a lady ain't gonna cry about them nice pretty little chickens being kilt by a miserable ole wild dog, I don't know what she *kin* cry about. And we'll find us a way to git shed of that ole wild dog before he do any more depperdation."

"Yes, we must." Mother pushed her hair back briskly, rose and looked through the window at the chickens wandering aimlessly in the dusty yard. "Those chickens represent the only money we can lay our hands on, because the cotton isn't going to bring a thing this year even if we can get it picked. And we have to have enough money to buy you some shoes, Unc' Alec. You can't work outside in the wintertime with no shoes."

"Oh, yas'm, I kin," Unc' Alec protested

blithely. "Shoes don't mean nothing to me. Cept'n for church," he added wistfully.

"You are going to have shoes," Mother said firmly. "And Nellie has to have shoes. It will soon be so nobody can go barefoot, and her shoes were already too little last year. She can hand them down to Bet, and Bet give hers to Maggie, and so on; and thank goodness, the baby will be in the cradle till winter's over. But Nellie must and shall have new ones. I could hand her down a pair of mine, if I had more than this one pair left." Mother laughed and stretched out her shabby little shoe with an almost roguish look of pleasure in the smallness of her foot.

Nellie felt ten-year-old pride in the bigness of *her* foot. Everybody was in birthday mood again. Mother was so wonderful. She was even wonderfuler than Rowena or Rebecca or any other of Scott's ladies. Nellie bet to herself that Rebecca couldn't tend to babies and animals and chickens and work about a hundred hours a day and still be pretty and laughing like Mother.

"I bet," said Nellie. "I bet——"

"Father thinks that is a feeble way to say I *believe,* Nellie," reminded Mother.

"Yes, but I do bet—I do believe—if we

59

could kill that old dog, and we ought to do it because he doesn't belong to anybody, and I bet—no,
believe—he must be ruining things for other people
too, and he's just a wild beast really, not a dog at
all," Nellie said in a rush.

"Well, what do you bet? Believe, I
mean," Mother said with a serious air of attention
that enchanted Nellie.

"I believe we could take his old yellow
skin to the shoemaker and get us some shoes made."

"Do you know," said Mother, "I believe
we could," and she gave Nellie the same look she
used to give Father, one compounded of pride and
admiration and love.

"Well, let's," Nellie said loudly. Then
she rose to pace the floor, hands behind her back,
just the way Father used to walk up and down out
in his study when he was making up a sermon. Especially when he was making up those last ones back
in 1860 when he was telling his people that the Union
must be preserved and we mustn't let the hotheads
rush us into things. Nobody liked those sermons,
though they loved Father so much they didn't say so.
And of course, after South Carolina seceded, Father
knew, and said, everybody had to be loyal to his State
and fight for it. Because one's State has to come first,

after God. But all these sermons took a lot of pacing up and down in the study, and you could see Father was thinking so hard it hurt. So now Nellie held her hands behind her back and walked up and down the same way, while Mother looked on and smiled, but rather dimly.

"I know what," Nellie pronounced. "Remember Father's old shotgun? He left it locked up in the study with some shots in it in case the Yankees came. You can unlock the study and Unc' Alec can take the gun and go shoot that yellow dog."

Unc' Alec almost jumped off the floor. "No, lil miss, I cain't do that," he pleaded. "Ole Alec cain't shoot anything."

"Of course you can, Unc' Alec," said Mother. "I'm sure you are a good shot."

"I don' know about that, ma'am," quavered Unc' Alec. "But I shore know I cain't shoot anything."

"Why can't you shoot that mean old dog, Unc' Alec?" asked Mother.

"Yes, why?" put in Nellie, stopping her pacing to stare at the old man in a way her mother had taught her never to look at grown people.

"I cain't kill *nothing*, Miss Margaret. The Good Book say, 'Thou shalt not kill,' don't it?

61

I cain't rightly do it. No, ma'am, I have to refuse,
ma'am."

"I never heard of such a thing," Nellie
cried indignantly. "Do you think you know more

what's right than our father? He's off killing Yankees every day of his life."

"Yes, ma'am, I know it, and that's all right. Your father such a good man he kin kill yaller dogs or Yankees or whatever thing he think oughter be kilt, and it'll be all right with the Lord, 'cause the Lord He know your father well, all this praying and preaching of his He done listened to all these years. He understand anything your father does and know it's right, even if the Good Book say not to, 'cause Cap'n Thomas is about the best man the Lord has made yit. But I ain't a good man. I'm a pore miserable sinner, bless Gawd, and I cain't kill nothing. Not nothing," he said with finality.

Nellie started arguing loudly, but her mother stopped her. "Don't, dear," she said. "It is wrong to persuade people against their convictions. We'll find another way. Maybe some man will stop by in a day or two, and we can get him to do it."

"Nobody ever stops by here, and besides in a day or two all the chickens will be gone," Nellie said bitterly.

"All the same, we can't make Unc' Alec do what he thinks is wrong. Now let's forget it for a while," said Mother firmly, and went out to the kitchen.

Nellie went into the shabby sitting room, picked up the basket of mending her mother entrusted to her, and started sewing viciously. She kept thinking of the chickens and shoes they were losing through Unc' Alec's scruples. She didn't see what old people needed with consciences when life was almost over.

The more she thought the sillier it all seemed. Ever since the beginning of time, men had fought and overcome the brainless forces that threatened them; she knew that from Father. And this old wild dog was like the dragons in the fairy tales Mother used to have time to read to her and Bet and Maggie, just something evil to be overcome by good. She *knew* Father would shoot the wild dog that harried the neighborhood. But Father wasn't here. What was to be done with Father not here?

Almost as clearly as in a vision (because of course remembrance of things in real life is never so clear as visions) she saw her father again as she had seen him one night at a "family dining," as he had called them, at Bruton's Fork. That was not long before the War. She had been taken along and put to bed upstairs with several of her cousins and two little colored girls to watch them. The little colored girls had fallen asleep, and she had crept

64

midway down the curving staircase and sat there listening to the grown people. There had been lots of talk, but all she remembered was something her father had said, standing as always with his hands behind him, in front of the fire, and looking so tall, so handsome with his springing crest of hair. She knew he was changing some quotation maybe, because she heard that chuckle of his, but also she heard him serious when he said it: "Let me have noble sons and stalwart daughters."

She thought of that now. Ever since that time, without knowing what stalwart was, she had wanted to be a stalwart daughter. Now that she was ten and with lots of reading behind her, she had an idea what stalwart meant. Certainly it meant not being afraid of a yaller dog when one's father was off fighting Yankees, and them with much more of everything than he: food, and clothing, and especially bullets.

"Father, I *am* stalwart. I'm not afraid of a yaller dog, nor an old gun," she said aloud, but more to herself than to him.

After that, it was a matter of minutes to go take the study key from where she always knew Mother had it, under the handkerchiefs in her second drawer, to go boldly out to the study, since

Mother at that time of day was always out in the kitchen, unlock the study door and go in. But it was not a matter of minutes to take that fearful gun away from the corner it stood in, festooned with cobwebs. Nellie stood still for some time, gathering courage. Although the room was hot beyond belief, locked up so long, and there was something making her want to cry about seeing Father's books on the shelves and him not in front of them looking at her with that quizzical loving smile she believed belonged only to her, she stood there for many minutes before she grabbed the gun and dragged it from its corner.

Then she gave in to her sense of drama, which was always strong, and addressed the empty room:

"Father, I can't tell if it's what you want, with Unc' Alec and the Bible confusing me, but I think you meant it about the stalwart daughters and I *think* this is being stalwart. You know I never even killed a mouse before."

She shuddered, remembering how there was always some laughing, kind colored person to come in from the Quarters and tend to things when her mother, mostly from hearsay, had announced a mouse or bat or spider or something like that in the

Big House, and how she had never really seen anything killed.

    She dragged the hideous shotgun across
the dusty floor, into the back yard, then, as fast as
she could go under such a tremendous weight, to
a corner of the smokehouse that gave view of the
chicken yard but couldn't be seen from the house.

    I may have to wait here hours, she
thought grimly. She leaned back against the smokehouse, squeezing under the overhanging shingles of
the roof so as to get out of the sun, though as she
was already freckled as a guinea egg, according to
Aunt Dozy, it couldn't do much more harm. She
could hear Maggie and Bet and Little William calling doodlebugs under the front steps and envied
them the cool as she shook her head to keep the per-
spiration out of her eyes. She stood first on one bare
foot and then the other, trying to ease the feeling of
weight that seemed to have gone from the gun to
her stomach; then she took to scratching her legs alternately with her toenails, because the mosquitoes
naturally took advantage of her motionlessness and
her too-short skirt. Then she tried to divert herself
by reciting in a whisper the last poem she had
learned for Friday-recitation day at the Academy,

but as it happened to be "The Bivouac of the Dead," and she was always greatly affected by her own renditions, she had to stop after the first couple of verses. "Wanter ruin your aim?" she muttered angrily to herself, brushing away the tears that always came with that poem, unless of course she was saying it in public.

So she tried "Little Giffen of Tennessee," a new poem which so fired her martial spirit that before she knew it she was saying it almost loud-

ly and in a marching tone which took so much of her energy that she pretty nearly failed to see a yellow shape that was suddenly behind a fig tree just beyond the chicken yard. But she did see it. Then she watched the gaunt yellow shape flatten itself under the chicken wire, and stand motionless and evil inside the chicken yard. The weight in her stomach became a twinge that threatened to double her up,

but she was able to pull the gun to her shoulder. Her fingers were shaking so she almost couldn't catch hold of the trigger, but she did. Then she turned the barrel on the dog. He just stood there. He was looking at her, and she knew she had never seen anything so wicked as his face. But it was heartbreaking too; surely a dog couldn't be so wild and unhappy that he looked more wolfish than a wolf. And perhaps if he were let to live and the War ever got over, he would get to be a decent dog again. And also she had heard so many sermons, though not from Father, about what happened to people who died in the midst of their sin. . . .

"I can't do it," she moaned.

She shut her eyes for an instant to see if he wouldn't go away. When she opened them, he was still there, stiff-legged and ready to spring. So she aimed the barrel at a point just beneath the wicked eyes. She wasn't conscious of pulling the trigger, but all of a sudden there was a crash. Judgment Day, she recognized at once. The skies fell, and the world came to an end.

It was resurrected, though, in a minute— the same world of back yard and chickens, only now the chickens were flapping and squawking, and so was Aunt Dozy, and Mother and Unc' Alec were bending over her, and there in the corner of the chicken yard lay a vile and piteous yellow body. Nellie turned her head away from the sight into Mother's shoulder. Then she remembered she was stalwart and got to her feet. She looked at the poor old wild dog with what she hoped was stalwart calm, and said, "Well, we've got that done, Mother."

"Oh, Nellie, my little brave Nellie!" cried her mother, who was very white but not so white as Unc' Alec was gray in the face.

Nellie would have broken down and wept at the praise, knowing how really scared she had been, except that her mother saw the danger and hastily went on in her brightest voice, "And now our poor chickens are safe. And now you and Unc' Alec shall have beautiful shoes."

"Oh, Mother, do you think Father will think I am stalwart?"

"Why, Nellie, he'll think you are the stalwartest daughter a father ever had!"

"But, *please,* Mother, you'll give me your old shoes and wear the ones made out of . . . made out of . . ."

"Indeed I will, dear," said Mother, who

71

hadn't been able to look at the corner of the chicken yard at all.

So Nellie's tenth birthday brought glory to her, and before long she really enjoyed looking at her mother's little feet in the dogskin boots.

III

Alexa Thomas McDonald's
tenth birthday

August 13, 1888

Alexa Thomas McDonald's

TENTH BIRTHDAY

August 13, 1888

O N ALEXA'S tenth birthday the McDonald family moved into their New House. And before noon that day it had become cruelly apparent to Alexa that not a soul remembered it was her birthday because of the excitement of finally settling into the House. The moving had been going on a long time before that; Alexa could hardly remember back to a time when the New House didn't absorb all their thoughts and furnish all their conversation—anyhow Ma's and Pa's and the girls'—and the actual moving had taken about a month, with mean old Jonas James coming every morning with his wagon and his nephew and carting off a few things. Ma had said to Pa, "That Prevatt crowd could do the moving in a day probably with all their wagons and men, but old Jonas James would die of jealousy since he moved us to this house when we got married. I suppose nobody would care much if he did die, whatever of," she said thoughtfully. "They say he beats his wife *terribly*, Duncan. But still I hate to hurt his feelings. So we'll let him take a few things every day; he hasn't the strength for more—I suppose he uses it up beating Rosy. And that way, moving will be so gradual, it won't be a shock to any of the children."

"Cutting off the dog's tail by inches," agreed Pa.

So that's the way they did it. Jonas James and his nephew, Major Gray James (named for his father's old master who got killed in the War) who stuttered so badly you never could know what he was saying, but it always sounded distressed no matter if he was grinning, would appear each morning before Ma could finish her coffee, though Pa would have cannily departed for the law office some time before. Then the house would be all morning a confusion of bumpings of furniture and snarlings of Jonas James and stutterings of Major Gray. They always managed to take just the things that couldn't be spared till the last moment, like Pearl's china painting set or the joggling board, and they even got as far as the gate with Pa's desk once, but Mammy saw them out of the upstairs window and hollered

them back. When Alexa or Pearl or Little-Nell ob-
jected to something of theirs being dragged away so
soon, old Jonas would fix whichever it was with his
beady eye and say, "Now, missy, you must don't want
me ever to finish thishere job. How you gonna live
in that fine new house if you don't let somebody
move you there?" Then he would shoulder whatever it was they were fussing about and throw it sav-
agely into the wagon.

      This went on for about a month, with
the old house looking a little sadder every day, until
finally they were all glad to leave it, even Little-Nell,
who said she liked it more than the New House and
always would. How Pearl and Alexa hooted when
Little-Nell said that! Little-Nell was often sorter
queer; she read poetry when she didn't have to, and
things like that; but even she had never said anything so downright crazy before. The idea of liking
a house that must be pretty near a hundred years old
and built of just wood better than a brand-new brick
house made from plans by a real architect, with a
piazza all around three sides and towers and turrets—
a mansion it was, because the *Marlboro County Advocate* said so: "The spacious brick mansion which
is being erected on West Main Street for our distin-
guished citizen, Mr. D. D. McDonald, is nearing com-

pletion." And now this last morning of the long move, with every book and toy and skillet finally gone, the old house looked as if it knew all about the spacious brick mansion and was brooding in quiet desperation; Alexa thought the brighter patches on the wallpaper where pictures used to hang made the sitting room look just as Pearl did when she was about to burst into tears, her face all mottled. But it was eight-year-old Little-Nell who did burst into tears as they filed out of the door and kept weeping till Pa took her hand and said, "Now dearie, now dearie."

"Oh, Pa," she cried, "here we're leaving, and I was just about to be able to reach the top of the mantelpieces. I've been waiting years till I would be tall enough to put things on the mantelpiece or take them off. And the mantelpieces here are so beautiful. All that carving. I can look at it like at pictures."

"But the mantels at the New House are so *elegant,* Ma says," put in Alexa comfortingly. "They are the very latest thing, with those posts going 'most to the ceiling and big looking glasses in between."

"Maybe so, but I can easily reach to the shelf part of *them,*" said Little-Nell. "I can even see

78

down past my nose in the looking glass. And I'd much rather be waiting for when I could reach to the dear old high mantels."

Pa laughed and patted her hand. "We mustn't underrate things just because they come easily, daughter. Lots of things will come easily to my girls, I hope," he said, looking with satisfaction at them as they walked down the shady street—Pearl (her real name was Margaret) tall and ladylike beside Ma, Alexa skipping with eagerness, though Hugh, two years older, stalked beside her with becoming nonchalance, and Little-Nell pale and wistful by his side, while the two little boys leaped and shouted on her heels.

"And I can see *all* my face in all the new mantelpiece mirrors," said Alexa, "and I like to."

"That's because you are so pretty!" burst out Little-Nell, who never stopped admiring Alexa, even when she quarreled with her, not often.

That somehow brought good humor to the whole group, and they strolled gently on down the dusty street, each thinking pleasantly about this great change, the girls, even Little-Nell, adventurously, Pa with serene satisfaction in what he was able to do for his family, and Ma in a state of vainglory which she had already admitted to herself and Pa.

79

Not the boys, though; Hugh was embarrassed at being part of what was undoubtedly a procession (he saw Mr. Hector Bounds and his colored man look satirically at them from the door of his blacksmith shop), and the little boys, Duncan and Kenneth, never thought about anything of course except what to eat or play next. Their steps quickened as they went through the big gate to the new place, and they went in a jubilant march along the walk that wound past the big magnolia tree and then lots of hydrangea bushes to the front steps. They stood for an instant on the front piazza looking out at the lawns with the big oak trees, some so big the three girls couldn't encircle them together, the great round bed of crimson salvia edged with purple ageratum in front of the house, the flower garden that stretched at the left of the house down to where the Baptist churchyard began, about a mile away, it seemed to Alexa; and best of all, the great mysterious cedar tree whose branches trailed to the ground to make a huge hidden playhouse underneath. Alexa sighed with anticipation; she was too old to play house now—even if nobody but her knew it—but she and Little-Nell could think of something grown-up enough for the tree house to be. A hiding place for Flora McDonald and Bonny Prince Charlie maybe.

Then Pa opened half of the big double front door that looked as if it belonged to a church and said just "Come in, come in." Pa never tried to sound important or even out of the ordinary, no matter what the occasion.

Ma swept in, like a queen entering her rightful domain, Alexa thought, and they followed, all silent—except of course for the little boys, who ran whooping out to the kitchen, acting as if everything were all new to them. And lots of things were. Ma and Pa had gone to New York City the month before, especially to get things for the new house, and since yesterday Jonas James and Major Gray and

probably some helpers had opened the huge crates from W. & J. Sloane and A. T. Stewart. So there the new things were, put in their places. And what things! First, in the hall a new hatrack, which looked exactly like a throne turning into an octopus; it was an oak seat you could sit on to put on rubbers but really a chest since the top lifted up, with carved arms and a looking glass for the back of the throne, going up about six feet and sprouting three times on each side to make hangers for hats and coats. There was nothing else in the big hall except an old half-table on which the inlay was pretty chipped, but Mittie had polished it till it shone like everything else, and above it an old dim mirror with a dilapidated eagle on top. But the chief thing in the hall was the staircase itself, going up and up with shining mahogany banisters that the little boys would keep shiny with the seats of their britches when Ma and Mammy weren't looking.

In the parlor was something that made even sophisticated fifteen-year-old Pearl gasp—a set of sofa and two chairs made of rich glistening mahogany carved in a marvelous confusion of roses and lilies and upholstered in green plush. There was a gentleman's armchair and a lady's armchair; nobody could decide which of the three pieces was the most beautiful; they were all *sumptuous*. They made the old Brussels carpet look rich too, and with the new curtains of gold brocade, the deep-green wallpaper with gold fleurs-de-lis, and gold shades on the gas chandelier that bloomed as unexpectedly in the middle of the room as mistletoe in a tree—well, as Pearl said, it was beyond words.

"Quite recherché," Ma pronounced, with calm satisfaction.

The new sideboard in the dining room was recherché too; oak, it was, with long-bearded heads carved on the doors which the little boys said were Santa Claus but which Alexa and Little-Nell found far from benign. *Everything* was recherché, whatever that meant—something deeply satisfying, Alexa could tell from Ma's look. The bowls and pitchers and other such things in every bedroom matching the wallpaper; the marvelous new thing called a telephone in the back hall; the delicious red damask curtains in the sitting room, which otherwise was all old, furnished entirely from the old house and "the nicest room of any," whispered Little-Nell to Alexa, who whispered back loyally, "But not elegant," though she felt suddenly happy to see all the old things together with nothing new to make them shamefaced.

But the best thing of all was yet to come. After they had looked at all the first floor including the back quarters with the kitchen and pantries full of all the most modern labor-saving devices, and a separate little roofed-over porch for the pump on one side of the back door and on the other a fine big milkhouse set in the ground with the roof made of slates and so low you could scratch pictures on the slates with a rock—after all that, Ma said, "Now for the surprise!" She led them back to the parlor and flung open the folding doors that led from it into the library. And there, glittering and gleaming against the brown of the wallpaper and Pa's brown law-books, was a piano, not a demure upright one like the old one, but a grand piano, standing there with its white teeth smiling and its wing poised for magnificent flight. While the girls gasped and fluttered, and Pa beamed, Ma sat down and dashed into the "March Militaire," sitting upright and commanding as if she had played at a grand piano all her life. But her face was pink as a rose, and when she finished with a crashing chord, she stood up, took Pa's arm, and looked from one to the other of them all as if she were shouting aloud the delicious triumph of a cherished woman.

But only for a moment. Then she said,

"Tut, this won't do. You girls go to your rooms and put everything in absolute order. There will be lots of things the colored people didn't know where to put. We must have our house perfect by our first suppertime, and it must be after three o'clock now."

They all dispersed, the girls to giggle and marvel upstairs with Mittie, who was newly acquired for the New House, their first maid; and Mr. McDonald to rescue his books that had been put in the glass bookcases upside down, and Mrs. McDonald to sit reposeful and proud on the green lady chair in the parlor, holding a volume of Browning's poetry which she was determined to understand some day, but certainly wasn't reading now.

She was still sitting there twenty minutes later with her eyes fixed on the same page and her thoughts jumping through every room in the house, landing on every new item with a positive bounce of pleasure, lingering luxuriously on the horsehair-filled cushions of the brand-new surrey in the barn and returning finally to the grand piano glowing in the next room, when they were suddenly summoned back by:

"Miss Nellie. Miss Nellie, you oughter be reading the Bible if you giving any book *that* much mind."

She looked up to see Mammy standing before her, trying with small success to look severe.

"Miss Nellie, we been sho-nuff having visitors out in the kitchen. I reckon everybody in town gonna have some business here in the kitchen till all of 'em see all these new things they hear about. Mis' Weatherly's butler got here soon as he finished milking their cow this morning, and I don't see how the Easterlings ever got their dinner, their Sarah here so long. She jes' hollered like she at a revival meeting when she see our refreezerator. Yes'm, jes' like a big meeting she wuz back there hollering."

Mrs. McDonald laughed. "Of course everybody wants to come see. You can give them all a cup of coffee and a rosette. Have you got some rosettes, or teacakes?"

"Miss Nellie, you know Rena made rosettes all afternoon yestiddy, in case of comp'ny. The pantry is plumb full of rosettes, lots of teacakes too, *and* wafers. I been giving 'em out like I knowed you'd want us to, but we got enough left to have a mighty big white folks' party today ef you wanted to."

Mrs. McDonald leaned back and closed her eyes at the thought.

"Now don't act like that, Miss Nellie.

Maybe in a minute you change your mind. What I come to tell you—the last person here to see us were Cap'n Bowman's coachman. He call himself coachman; he just their butler really, but he spend all the afternoons riding Mis' Bowman around leaving them little calling cards, so he think he can call himself coachman. Anyhow, he been here too."

Mrs. McDonald sprang to attention. Mrs. Bowman (Cap'n Mag, everybody called her—at a safe distance—because she talked so much about her husband's war record and was so obviously his superior officer) was Mrs. McDonald's enemy. Though Mrs. McDonald wouldn't admit as much, one of the chief joys of owning this new house, this palatial mansion, was to show Cap'n Mag that Captain McDonald, who never let anyone call him Captain now, was able to build for his wife a house with more turrets and towers than the one Captain Bowman had ensconsed Cap'n Mag in the year before.

"What did he come for?" she asked with elaborate lack of interest.

"He just stop to say he mighty surprised to see such a fine house here in Wes' Williamsville." She saw Mrs. McDonald's eyebrows flare, and hastily added, "He say we mighty lucky to work for such fine people in such a fine house. He say there ain't any

88

Philadelphia lawyer can law like Mr. McDonald. And he say there wouldn't be air' bank in this county if Mr. McDonald hadn't started one. And he say, last thing he hear, Mr. McDonald starting a railroad train coming here, and he president of it and gonna let us all ride anywhere we feel like."

"I don't know about that," began Mrs. McDonald.

"And more 'n that, he say to me Mis' McDonald a might nice lady to work for, when you think of some of 'em. He say just you think of some ladies and you see Mis' McDonald mighty easy to get along with." Mammy paused, conscious of the right word spoken.

Mrs. McDonald was unfeignedly smiling. "But is that all you came to tell me, Mammy? I'm glad your friends appreciate Mr. McDonald, but that isn't any reason to—to interrupt my reading," she said, picking up her book.

"No'm, I ain't come to tell you that. I know you already know Mr. McDonald a mighty fine man to work for and you a mighty fine lady and we sho does like this fine house we got now. What I want to tell you John William said was sump'n else. He said——" Mammy paused and cocked a wary eye at Mrs. McDonald.

"Well, what? Really, Mammy!" Mrs. McDonald, with a look of patience exhausted, made gestures of returning to an engrossing book.

"I tell you what." Mammy suddenly seemed to swell all over; this, as Mrs. McDonald and every child except possibly little Kenneth knew, was a sign of moral indignation; it made Mammy look twice her regular size. "I tell you what that John William say to me. He say Mrs. Bowman going right tomorrow morning and visit her sister in Columbia and stay there three weeks. And John William say he believe she just leaving town because she know you and Mr. McDonald and us soon be giving what he call a house-swarming party and ef she stay here she have to come to that party and hear all those people mirating about how much finer our house is than hern."

"Ha!" Mrs. McDonald exclaimed, then turned the sound into a refined cough. She composed her face to blankness, staring thoughtfully at Mammy, who continued to swell. Suddenly, in spite of all she could do in the way of compressing her lips, the expression that Little-Nell and Alexa called Ma's mischievous look invaded her face; her eyes sparkled, two little lines crinkled beneath them, her fringe sprang into livelier curls, her beaded slipper tapped the floor, and a humming like a mosquito's came from her lips. Mammy deflated a little at the rollicking sight.

"Mammy, go tell Mr. McDonald I said come here a minute."

"Yes, *ma'am.*" Mammy pushed open both the folding doors into the library—anybody else in the house could get through by pushing just one of the doors into the wall, but Mammy, as she proudly said herself, showed her keep.

"Mr. McDonald, Miss Nellie say will you kindly step into the poller for jes' a minute, suh?"

Mr. McDonald came at once, his finger still marking his place in the first book he had picked up in his rearranging project. He sat down in the gentleman armchair in his decisive way, twinkled at his pretty wife, and said, "Well, my love?"

"Duncan! That hateful Cap'n Mag Bowman! She's going off tomorrow morning to visit her sister in Columbia for three weeks!"

Mr. McDonald replied mildly, "My love, as I remember Cap'n—Mrs. Bowman's sister, I would call a visit to her distinctly Christian rather than hateful."

"Don't be dull, Duncan. You know she's

going away just to miss our housewarming reception because she'd be so mortified and chagrined to come and hear what everybody will be saying about this beautiful house."

"Are we having a housewarming reception?"

"Of course we are. Everybody expects it. I was going to speak to Cousin Molly Marsh tomorrow about making little cakes with flowers on them. And engage cream for the sillabub. We've got plenty of hens for the salad if Uncle Peter'll let us kill them, but that's all there is on the place for it. It would take me at least a week to get it all arranged. Just writing the invitations would take a day. I counted up and there are forty people we'll just have to have, besides the kin."

"That will make at least seventy people then. I shouldn't think you'd miss Cap'n—Mrs. Bowman in a crowd of that size."

"I certainly would. And I shan't let her get out of it," declared Mrs. McDonald. "You just listen to what I'm going to do."

Mammy leaned chortling over the sofa to listen to what Miss Nellie was going to do.

"I shall give the party this very afternoon."

92

Mammy gave a crow of joy, and Mr. Mc-Donald, imperturbable man, managed not to give a start.

"We can do it, can't we, Mammy?"

"We shore-god can, Miss Nellie, we shore can."

"I know you can do *anything,* my love, but is it worth while, all the commotion? Just to thwart Cap'n Mag?" asked her husband in his legal voice.

"It shore-god is!" declared Mrs. McDonald, then sprang to her feet beaming with energy and mischief. "Mammy, you run out and tell Mitchell to stop whatever he's doing in the yard and hitch up and drive out to Cousin Molly Marsh's and ask her please to make *thousands* of her best cheese straws; poor thing, she'll be so glad to earn the money she won't mind the rush. Tell her we'll send the carriage for her and the cheese straws at five o'clock. Oh, and, Mammy, go get my white kid gloves from my bureau drawer and wrap them up while I write a little note to say I hope she can use them because I have outgrown them. Poor thing, she had on cotton ones at Mrs. Everett's reception and looked so mortified!"

Then Mrs. McDonald spied Alexa coming slowly down the staircase. Alexa trailed one freckled hand elegantly down the mahogany banister—she was a princess indulgently watching her populace revel below in honor of her tenth birthday. Her mother's voice broke into the frenzied cheers that burst out when the adoring subjects realized she was coming down the palace steps.

" 'Lexa! Go tell Uncle Peter to come here, then run over to Aunt Sis's and ask if she'll lend us Old Joe for a couple of hours. Then call Pearl and Little-Nell and all of you pick all the flowers you can find and put them all over the house, even in the bedrooms and the nursery. But first all you girls come here and I'll tell you what."

Alexa was puzzled, but she knew when not to ask questions, and after receiving a reassuring nod from her father and seeing an amused smile in his beard, she flew to follow instructions. She felt the instructions had nothing to do with her birthday, but by this time she was beginning to enjoy her secret in a wry way. Fifteen minutes later she and Pearl stood, holding their harvest of flowers, before their mother, flushed from her foray into the pantry to marshal fifty wineglasses, and their Father, still smiling benignly and occasionally reading.

"Now girls," said Mrs. McDonald with

a sound she would have called a giggle if it had been one of them making it, "we are having a party at five o'clock this afternoon."

"Ma!" gasped Alexa. "What kind of a party?"

"An entirely new kind of party," Mrs. McDonald said. "An informal housewarming party. Just a minute, I'll tell about it," she said, seeing Uncle Peter and Old Joe standing in the parlor door, both their black faces gleaming with excitement— they had already heard more in the kitchen about her plans than she knew herself yet.

"Come here, youall," she said, and they

stood before her grinning happily at the chandelier and the new furniture, and looking ready for anything. "I want you each to go put on those shiny new white coats—Uncle Peter will give you one, Old Joe; you can turn up the sleeves till they fit. Then one of you start one end of town and the other one the other end, and go ring the doorbell at every one of my friends' houses—both of you know exactly who they all are—and ask to see the lady of the house. When she comes, make a nice bow and say, 'Mrs. So-and-so, Mr. and Mrs. McDonald just moved into their New House this morning, and they want to have a very informal gathering this afternoon so they can see their friends on the very first day of their New House. So will youall please give them the pleasure of your company at five-thirty this afternoon.' Now say that, every word. And if anybody should say they can't come, remember who it is so you can tell me. But," she added with serene conviction, "nobody will say that."

She made each of the old men say over this speech to her till she was satisfied, then sped them on their way. If she could have followed them and heard their zestful performance, she would have been disconcerted to see how much more accurately, if not more spiritedly, the borrowed butler gave her message than her own butler, because Old Joe repeated her every word, though not always with the same pronunciation, while Uncle Peter contented himself with "Howdy, miss. We moved into our New House today and Miss Nellie say for youall to come over to a mighty big party right this afternoon and she'll expect you at hap'pas' five and we hopes you'll git there." As Mrs. McDonald prophesied, everybody accepted, including Mrs. Bowman; there was no way out of it for her, and nobody else would have missed it for a bale of cotton.

When Old Joe and Uncle Peter had started on their rounds, Mrs. McDonald said to her gaping daughters, "You are each to put on your best—Pearl the yellow mull; Alexa, your sprigged muslin and be sure Mittie irons the sash; Little-Nell, your dotted swiss; and give your hair not less than a hundred licks with the brush, every one of you. Youall can help Uncle Peter and Old Joe hand the refreshments, only they won't need much help because there's no time to make sillabub or ice cream, so we'll just have that case of sherry wine your Father brought from New York City." She blandly did not see her husband wince at this, and continued, "It will be *most* sophisticated."

She thought a moment and added complacently, "It will probably start a new style in parties."

"I bet a lot of 'em will wonder where the chicken salad is, though," muttered Alexa, but that was just her forgotten birthday rankling in her; her ready imagination told her that in this party her irrepressible Mother was doing something very recherché indeed.

Pearl seized this favorable moment to further her own ends. "If it's a party to celebrate the house, Ma, why can't we invite a few young people too? The Campbells and the Macmillans maybe. And Judge Owens' nephew who's visiting him."

Mrs. McDonald gave such easy assent to this that Pearl pushed on. "And there's a young man I met at the Macmillans', you know he's nice if they invited him, and I saw him at the spelling match at the Academy last spring when he first came and he spelled everybody down, even Judge Owens, and he's so *romantic*-looking—such blue eyes you never saw—and he's so tall and stands straight as a prince and he is so poor and he ran away from home so as to earn money because they lost everything in the war and he learned how to mend watches and he sleeps in the back of his store and all the girls are crazy about him but he works too hard to go to many parties and I meant to ask you when you got back from New York if we couldn't invite him to supper sometime——"

"Duncan!" said Mrs. McDonald, "Who is this—person?"

"Well, my love, all I know about him seems to be good. He has started a savings account in the bank, I know. His name is Carroll and his home is in North Carolina."

"The name is all right, certainly, and while I don't think much of North Carolinians, after all I have to remember *you* are from there—so maybe North Carolinians are the best of all," said Mrs. McDonald judicially.

"Thank you, my love," said Mr. McDonald.

"But to ask a strange young man to an informal gathering of old friends—impossible!" said Mrs. McDonald, bending a queenly look on Pearl.

"Oh, Ma——" began Pearl.

But Mr. McDonald was talking, in his unhurried way. "And Captain Jacob Bowman was telling me the other day that he and Captain Mag—he and Maggie had invited this young man to Sunday dinner because Jacob and the young man's father had been in the same company and went through

Gettysburg together. Unfortunately, the young man was unable to accept."

"Oh," said Mrs. McDonald. "I am sure," she added thoughtfully after a pause, "it is our duty to be kind to strangers if we know who they are. Let us hope, though," she said with one eyebrow threatening, "that he isn't too busy to come *here.*"

"Oh, *Ma!*" squealed Pearl.

"Restrain yourself, Pearl. And go find Mitchell's son and send him here, and I will send him to go invite the young people—what a pity nobody but us has one of those telephones; that would make it so easy. I shall send a note to young Mr. Carroll since we don't know him, and Mitchell's son is so lacking he can't give a message. The other young people will know what he is saying because I'm sure news of the party is all over town by now."

Then she turned to Alexa, who had been listening but was profoundly uninterested, maybe even a little bitter, to hear Pearl's plans going forward so smoothly when it was supposed to be *her* big day.

"Now whom shall we invite for you, dear? Ellen Townsend?"

"No'm. I'll just watch the others." Alexa would have gloried in having Ellen Townsend, but Ellen knew it was her birthday and might say something about it, and Ma would be so mortified. Alexa would just have to look on at the party without a companion, and tomorrow lead Ellen to believe the birthday celebration had happened beforehand.

"How about you, Little-Nell?" asked Mrs. McDonald with an indulgent smile.

"No'm. Not enough to eat for any of my friends, and I'd rather just watch the grown people."

"Very well. Then everybody scatter and get to work. Pearl, you arrange the flowers—you have an artistic touch. Alexa, you make sure there isn't a spot of dust anywhere for Mrs. Bowman to put her white glove in. Little-Nell, you keep the little boys happy, and make sure Hugh washes before the company comes. Only about an hour to go."

The girls moved to the door, Pearl planning to apply curlpapers before starting on the flowers, Little-Nell composing a poem in her head which had already started, "This is the birthday of a house," but surely need not go on, "So far we haven't seen a mouse," which was all she could think of. Alexa was thinking of nothing, through self-discipline; no use to think of an ignored tenth birthday. She paused at the door and looked back at her mother, who gave her a smile with bird-bright eyes.

"Isn't this a wonderful day?" said her mother to Alexa alone, since Mr. McDonald was again deep in *Coke upon Littleton*.

"Yes'm," said Alexa and closed the door gently.

We will pass over the next hour, since none of that family would like you to know of all the work done, getting the house and refreshments ready. In that part of the country, to this day, work is like ill-health: it is engaged in when unavoidable, but always secretly. So we will not look at Mrs. Mc-Donald polishing glasses furiously while she called directions about paprika and such to Mammy and Mittie and Rena as they deviled eggs and made sandwiches, or sent word to Mitchell's son to stop sweeping the spotless front walk and go hang the curtains in the rose room; or at the girls rushing about armed with dust rags against Mrs. Bowman's white gloves while they kept the little boys happy and out of the way and restrained them from eating the refreshments as fast as these were ready.

Instead we will skip to about six o'clock when the party was in full swing; that is to say, every room was swarming with people and Mrs. Bowman had arrived, carefully late. She was now looking very gloomy and apparently unimpressed by any of the grandeurs of hall, parlor, library, dining room, and mother-and-father bedroom. Mrs. McDonald had engaged her sister, the children's Aunt Sis, to escort Mrs. Bowman through these rooms and make her take in their glories, but not to let her wander into the sitting room with its relics of a humbler past. Then she was to take Mrs. Bowman up the massive stairs and confront her with the matching wallpapers and washstand sets, not to mention the new brass beds. But Mrs. Bowman, after the hatrack and the sideboard and the telephone ("For goodness' sake, hasn't Nellie got enough noise from all these children without bringing in more?") and the piano and the parlor set, had balked at the foot of the stairs and, after rubbing her gloved hand wistfully and unavailingly on the elaborate stair post, flatly refused to go up.

"I wouldn't climb up those stairs to see Queen Victoria's bedroom," she announced. "Alexa's bedroom down here is mighty fine, almost as big as mine, and of course she's got that dressing room too. I don't quite see the use of it, but I expect some people would think it was mighty elegant."

She was now sitting, still unimpressed, on the lady armchair in the parlor, apparently impervious to the babble of admiration going on around her. She was gazing distrustfully at the glass of sherry she held and talking to Mr. Brooks Hibbard, who owed Captain Bowman six months' rent for his warehouse and was hovering gallantly (grimly, though, Alexa thought), proffering little sandwiches without their tops, as daringly proposed by the *Ladies' Home Journal,* and having them waved away by a supercilious white glove. What she was talking to him about (Alexa by straining her ears could hear) was how she had never before been to a party where there was no real collation.

"I keep hearing people say how stylish this is," she was saying in her little waspish voice. "But what I say is, style don't fill your stomach. That's what I'll tell Nellie tomorrow—style don't fill you up like chicken salad and sillabub."

Alexa flushed, suddenly realizing that eavesdropping was contemptible, especially when you heard things you didn't like, and was about to move out of earshot of Cap'n Mag when she became aware of a young man standing before her, a young man so straight and tall and so blue-eyed that she realized instantly that he must be the Mr. Carroll

Pearl had managed to get invited by grace of Pa and of Mrs. Bowman's unaccepted invitation.

He was smiling at her. He said, "How do you do? I know you are Miss Alexa. Could I sit beside you for a minute and tell you how pretty your new house is?"

Alexa moved over to the sofa and sat gazing dumbly as he sank down beside her with the look of one who would like a few moments' peace. There was something in his grave look that made her think to herself that he might be as good a companion at just looking on as Ellen Townsend would have been. And he looked as if he would never hear Mrs. Bowman's remarks, all subtly directed against Ma, even if they were shouted in his ear.

She sat silent, smiling back at him, then bethought herself of her duties as daughter of the house. She tried to think of some small talk, gave a few seconds' thought to what Ma or even Pearl, who was already clever at this sort of thing, would say, then, unknowingly indicating the skilled hostess she was to become, plunged into a subject she was really interested in.

"You spelled down Judge Owens, didn't you?"

He laughed, and suddenly showed himself as the eighteen-year-old boy he was underneath all the gravity and poise of a young man earning his way in a strange place.

"Yes. I was so surprised. But I do read a lot, and I reckon the look of the words gets into your mind. Do you like spelling?"

"Yes, I think so." Alexa stopped to think some more and make sure; then she smiled all over her face, the way her mother sometimes did. "I'm

106

sure I do, because it's about the only thing I do better than Pearl and Little-Nell. I don't read much though, mostly *Elsie Dinsmore,* but I do know how to spell. That's a good thing too, because it's all I can do better than Pearl. She can draw and paint and embroider and play the piano a little and make biscuits. And Little-Nell can make up poems. It makes me awfully glad I can spell. Pa says anybody who can spell shows he respects words. He says that so often that sometimes I think he is thinking about how I'm not really as smart as the other two girls."

Mr. Carroll did not laugh but his eyes became even bluer as he said in an even gentler voice than his regular one, which sounded like music even when he just said how-do-you-do, "I don't think that is what he is thinking, because he is a very wise man— everybody knows that—and he knows all the things each of you has that the other two haven't."

Alexa thought that over, then asked, "What have I got?"

"Well, of course I don't really know you girls yet, so I can't make any comparisons, but I'd be willing to bet, if I had any money to bet with, that few people your age have as much natural kindness and interest in dealing with strangers as you have. That amounts to a talent, you know. Just from seeing them here today, I don't believe Miss Pearl or Miss Little-Nell have that talent for people, though they maybe talk more."

Alexa glowed.

"Also," he went on, "but this is less important, when you look in your looking glass about three years from now, when you'll be interested in doing so, you'll see you've got something very valuable because it's mighty scarce. That's beauty. And it'll be yours forever, if the other things, the kindness and interestedness, you know, don't change. And it will make lots of people, especially one person, mighty happy. There, I sound like a Sunday-school superintendent, don't I? That's your penalty for being young. People talk at you. How old are you, Miss Alexa?"

"Ten."

"I thought so—maybe a little younger or maybe a little older."

"No, ten exactly, as exactly as you can get it. Shall I tell you a secret?"

"If you really want to. Being told secrets is something I'm mostly a little scared of."

"It's something I wouldn't usually think of doing—telling one, I mean." Alexa thought that over, and found out what was moving her. "You are different. The secret is: today is my birthday, my tenth birthday."

"Oh, happy birthday!" His eyes were bluer than ever. "But why is it a secret?"

"Because everybody has forgotten it but me. Maybe I should have reminded Ma, because she would be mortified and chagrined to think she had forgotten. But she has been so busy. You can't think how busy, all this moving. I was going to remind her this afternoon when we were plumb in the New House, but this party came along."

"I see." And Alexa could tell he did; he would always see everything.

"You know that's one of the things we like best about my ma. She always puts all her mind on one thing, and sometimes it is so funny and, you know, sweet. When she gets a new piece of music f'instance, or a new book, she doesn't think about a thing else all day. And this house moving—she hasn't thought about a thing else for a month, with old Jonas being so aggravating. And then today this party came along, and she hasn't been able to think about anything but having it and making Cap'n Mag Bowman come to it when she didn't want to."

Mr. Carroll threw back his head and laughed. When he laughed you could see he was somewhere sad underneath, but you could see also he wasn't thinking about himself as most people were.

"Well, I believe that was a good cause," he declared.

"And of course the thing is, when Ma is in one of her spells of thinking about just one thing, the thing is just as liable as not to be *you,* and that's lovely."

"It is," agreed Mr. Carroll. "But isn't your mother apt to be distressed from time to time about the things she has overlooked when her mind was on one thing? Like forgetting your birthday, for instance?"

"Oh, yes. I worried about that. And like I told you, I was going to tell her about it this afternoon, but the party happened. I'll tell her, as if I just remembered about it, in a day or two when we are settled down here."

"Well, I'm not too sure it'll be the same. I expect she likes to please you and make a lot of your birthday," said Mr. Carroll, smiling into the vivid little face.

"Of course she does. She'd rather please Pa or one of us than anything," Alexa said proudly.

110

"Of course," said Mr. Carroll in a matter-of-fact way which proved he hadn't heard that quaver in her voice. "And I know you'll enjoy your birthday when it is celebrated."

He was fumbling in the pocket of his shabby suit. "Look, Miss Alexa, would you allow me to give you a present, even if we are such new friends—I have a feeling we are going to be old ones someday? And it isn't really a present, and you probably won't have much use for it because all you can do with it is put keys on it, I reckon, but I had a little strip of silver and I took to playing with it at my workbench yesterday and I thought it made a pretty little trinket so I put it in my pocket, and if you like it, I'd like mighty well to have you accept it. I would feel it an honor."

Alexa's face pinkened at these courtly words addressed to her, and when he put in her hand a perfect little heart made of silver, her own heart thought it would burst with pleasure.

"Oooh" was all she was able to say, but Mr. Carroll could see what all she meant, because his own face grew radiant too.

Just then there was a rustle of skirts and a whiff of cologne, and Ma herself stood before them, looking regal in her puce silk but somehow still mischievous, as she gently waved in front of a flushed triumphant face the ivory fan Pa had given her last anniversary.

"Darling, do go tell Uncle Peter to fill Mrs. Bowman's glass before she gets to the bottom," she instructed with a chuckle. "And, Mr. Carroll, do sit down again and tell me how you like South Carolina," she commanded, sinking with a final rich rustle onto the sofa.

"Thank you, ma'am, I like it very much," said Mr. Carroll, bringing his blue gaze back from Alexa, who disappeared into the hall, and fixing it on Mrs. McDonald. "People have certainly been kind to me. Like your inviting me here for this—this happy occasion."

"It *is* a happy occasion," agreed Mrs. McDonald, her eyes fixed on Mrs. Bowman across the room, who seemed to be finding the lady armchair uncomfortable and to be spreading the discomfort to the grimly faithful Mr. Brooks Hibbard.

Mr. Carroll took counsel with himself for an instant, then said clearly, "A doubly happy occasion, I gather."

"Doubly?" repeated Mrs. McDonald, wondering if he was one of those tiresome modern young people you had to dig out meanings from and then often as not find them not meanings at all but just a stylish way of talking.

"Well, I kinder gathered that this was not only youall's first day in your new house but Miss Alexa's tenth birthday as well." Mr. Carroll stopped, bravely smiling but wondering if he had overstepped.

"*What!*" exclaimed Mrs. McDonald. "Could this be August the thirteenth already? Goodness gracious sakes!"

She sat immersed in thought for a moment, then rose to her feet. "*Thank* you, Mr. Carroll," she said with the same whole-face smile Alexa had given him. "Now I must leave you. There are things to be seen to in the kitchen. But first let me introduce you to Mrs. Bostwick. She's the mother of lots of nice young people. They live out in the country and give lovely parties."

This introduction she accomplished with as much swiftness as grace; then she disappeared.

Ten minutes later Mr. Carroll was still talking with Mrs. Bostwick, who had four young-lady daughters and so was very vivacious with young men, when Mr. McDonald appeared in the doorway and, to everyone's surprise, considering what a retiring sort of man he was, rapped on the doorframe for attention. He was beaming as no one there had ever seen him beam before.

"Ladies and gentlemen," he called so they could hear him in all the rooms, "Uncle Peter and Old Joe will see that your glasses are filled, and

then will you please move into the dining room to drink a toast?"

Uncle Peter and Old Joe moved about the rooms pouring sherry and grinning and spilling. Then Mr. McDonald took Alexa's hand as she stood

puzzled beside him, and together they led the wondering crowd into the dining room. There stood Ma
waiting, positively wreathed in smiles, with Hugh
and Pearl and Little-Nell and the little boys drawn
up beside her. And on the table stood that pound-
cake Cousin Molly Marsh had brought along just in
case but Ma had told her wouldn't be sophisticated
enough to serve with sherry wine. It was a great
white monument of a cake and now it had been
transformed with ten lighted candles. The crowd of
people pushed in, ohing and ahing, even Cap'n Mag
Bowman, and when they had got quiet enough,
Mr. McDonald raised his glass and said in his deep
voice, "My friends, you have come to rejoice with
us in our New House. Now I ask you to rejoice
with us in something much more important—our
dear daughter's tenth birthday. To Alexa!"

Then everybody drank. Alexa had never
before in her life felt so proud and important. Imagine people like Judge Owens and Dr. Vernon and
the head of the Academy drinking a health to *her!*
She felt her eyes sting with happy tears, but managed to raise her head and stammer, "Oh, thank
you!" looking around the room at these suddenly
dear people and finally resting her bemused eyes on
the quiet blue gaze of Mr. Carroll.

116

After all the party were gone, everyone giving a handshake to Alexa as well as to Ma and Pa and some of them saying positively embarrassingly nice things to her, there were presents. Hugh gave her a rather dog-eared copy of *Peck's Bad Boy and His Pa,* Kenneth gave her his best bottle-horse made from a green bottle instead of the usual brown and with an extra long string to pull it with, and Duncan gave her a penny. Pearl gave her two handkerchiefs, beautiful though a little dusty in the folds, and Little-Nell gave her a poem, very straggly and blotchy, saying

> Happy birthday, Alexa.
> You are the elixir
> Of life to all you meet
> Because you are so sweet,

which Pa said was a masterpiece of intellect as well as of truth. And Pa gave her ten whole shining silver dollars. And Ma, bursting into tears and laughter because she was so pleased and maybe relieved at the happy birthday, gave her the golden bracelet Pa had given her when Alexa was born. All these things Alexa put in a row on the mantelpiece of her pink-and-white new room when she went to bed. The little silver heart she slipped under her pillow.

IV

Alexa McDonald Carroll's
tenth birthday

February 4, 1914

Alexa McDonald Carroll's

TENTH BIRTHDAY

February 4, 1914

Fᴵᴿˢᵀ crack that morning 'Lexa wished it wasn't her tenth birthday. What was the use of having a birthday when Mamma wasn't at home? And when you couldn't even comfort yourself as you usually could when she was away by thinking anyhow she was off in New York with Papa having a good time and also buying dozens of train presents. This time she was 'way off in Canada with Aunt Pearl who lived up there and had had an operation and thought it would be cheering to have Mamma there to talk about Marlboro County.

Mamma hadn't really wanted to go 'way off up there in the dead of winter. She had kept thinking how Papa would probably catch his death of cold, staying so late uptown Saturday nights because she wasn't home that his fire would go out—he'd never notice because he would be so taken up with the renters' troubles. And thinking maybe Jander would come home from college and her not there. And thinking how Nell would be having examinations at the high school and need somebody to go over her Latin with her. And thinking how Wyndol and Duncan would stay up too late. And the three youngest children would catch measles or something.

Also, 'Lexa was pretty sure, thinking how she hated to be away for 'Lexa's birthday, though that wasn't mentioned by either of them. In fact, in spite of knowing Mamma wouldn't for the world be away on a child's birthday if she could help it, 'Lexa was a little hurt that she said nothing about it when she was dreading the trip because of the other things like Papa's catching the cold.

Well, anyhow, Mamma was gone, and everything about the day was going to be dreadful. To begin with, 'Lexa looked out the window and saw that the lovely, miraculous film of snow which had fallen last night was all melted. The children had gone to bed sure that it would keep snowing and that Papa would telephone the rest of the Board and say let's call off school today so the young people can frolic in the snow. And there was nothing but mud. She reckoned that was a sign how the whole day would be.

122

February 4, 1914

When Howard came tipping in to make her fire, she startled him by saying over her mound of bedclothes, "Howard, you know what?"

He knew the answer, "Stick your head in the hominy pot," but didn't say it of course; that would be sassy. He said, "You 'wake might early, Miss 'Lexie. Is you sick?"

"No. But it's my birthday, and Mamma's not here," said 'Lexa, trying hard to sound simply explanatory.

"Thass the truth," Howard responded sympathetically. "But she didn't aim to be away on your birthday—if she had her ruthers, she's be right here. But when a sister want something, a person have to do it."

"And nobody knows it's my birthday, and I ain't going to tell them. Think how mortified Nell would be if she knew it at the last minute and hadn't done anything about it."

She thought rather pleasurably about Nell's being mortified (and chagrined: Mamma always said the two words together as *her* mother used to do), then added, "And you *know* Papa don't know when our birthdays come without Mamma here to tell him."

"Thass the truth," Howard agreed. "I

reckon you better jes' not say nothing today, and when your ma gets home she mought have the birthday another day."

"No," said 'Lexa firmly and, she thought, magnificently. "I guess lots of people go without birthdays."

"They sho do," said Howard. "Fur's I rickollict, I ain't never had one till I come here."

He soliloquized comfortingly on the unnecessity of birthdays till he had finished his fire, then left. 'Lexa lay in bed as usual to wait for the room to get warm, and spent the time feeling rather noble but still a little cross with her unremembering brothers and sisters, until she fell asleep again. She woke suddenly at a call from Easter in the downstairs hall, "You 'Lexie, what ail you? The others 'most through breakfast," and jumped out of bed feeling cross with herself now as well as with her family. She was going to be tardy again.

The rest of the children had gone to school when she clumped downstairs. She felt uncomfortable because one of her face stockings was fastened to her underbody with just one button ("Mamma being off means buttons being off, too," she thought with grim humor), and also her hair parting was in the wrong place and hurt. She didn't

feel any better when Easter said, "Is you washed your face? I declare you don't look like somebody with a—like somebody oughter look to go to school."

And the cocoa had skins in it and the biscuits were pretty near stone-cold and the hominy had lumps and the sausage had so much red pepper she felt it clear up to the hurting part in her hair.

And when she got to school puffing, she was five minutes late, and Miss McCarley raised her eyebrows and said, "Tardy again?" without smiling. And just as she slid into her desk, she heard a "pop" and then saw the one button that was holding up her left stocking go rolling across the floor. It landed at that hateful Frank Malden's feet and he picked it up and showed it to Jack Odom and they both leered at her.

That was bad enough, but then of course she had to hold up one finger "to be excused," and Miss McCarley really frowned at her as she moved gingerly out of the room, holding her knees together so as to keep her stocking from falling and making her disgrace complete. She hobbled down to the girls' basement and started working on her stocking. She tried over and over to twist it around beneath her knee and tuck in the top, as she had seen Nell do with lisle stockings, but no use. Nobody, least of all poor fumbling 'Lexa, could tuck in the top of a face stocking.

She was standing in despair beyond tears, knowing she would just have to stay there all day, when rescue came—in the person of Honey-May Adams of all people. Honey-May was her enemy— by inheritance, because Honey-May was in her cousin

126

Marjie's grade and Marjie hated her—at least she hated her as much as Marjie could hate anybody. So 'Lexa did too, and 'Lexa rather enjoyed hating people, anyhow sneaky, whispering ones like Honey-May Adams. She couldn't bring herself to speak to Honey-May, but stood there so hopeless and still that Honey-May exclaimed, "What's the matter with you?"

'Lexa told her about the stocking, and first Honey-May laughed, but then 'Lexa looked so pale that she said, "I'll fix it, just wait," and ran up the basement stairs and down the hall to the first grade where Miss Henning always had bandages and quinine and such, and came back with a huge safety pin.

"There, pin it to your underbody," she said, "and it'll be all right."

She started to smile reassuringly. Then apparently she remembered about Marjie and her being enemies. She said in a mocking voice, "You won't be able to walk so uppity today, though!" and ran back upstairs before 'Lexa could say thank you even.

The rest of the day was just like that. Fitty Smithers, who sat in front of 'Lexa and was fat, so terribly fat it made you feel a little sick just to look at him even when he was all right, had one of his fits during geography and, before Mr. Miller and one of the high-school boys could get him out, had thrashed around so that lots of ink splashed out of 'Lexa's inkwell even through the iron top and soaked through the composition on Lincoln she had just finished copying.

She was sorry about the fit; no matter how often Fitty's fits happened, her spine melted away in the same sick pity. But after he was gone and she remembered that he would be back unperturbed in a short while, she was even sorrier about the composition, six long pages, the longest she ever wrote. That was because while she was writing it she suddenly got a feeling that maybe Lincoln wasn't so bad after all, and had decided to find out all she could about him— she even went to the library and looked in books. Then she had written and written, and actually had a good time doing it. She had copied over all she had written, feeling quite surprised at how good it was and how full of lovely long words, and the copying took forever because she did it in the most rigorous Palmer writing. Her arm was sore from it. In Palmer writing you wrote without moving your fingers, moving your whole arm from the fat part below the elbow resting on the desk, and, according to the red *Palmer Writing Book*, it was the "modern effortless method"; but all that effortlessness left you plumb tired and sore, especially if the teacher was looking on and you didn't get a chance to wiggle your fingers once in a while. And now there were six pages of Palmer writing to be done at once.

So, instead of going out to recess, 'Lexa asked if she could stay in and copy "Lincoln" over and Miss McCarley agreed, with her first real smile of the day. That smile made 'Lexa feel better. At least until spelling lesson. That should have been fun, because 'Lexa was almost always the last one up; the room had got so they all expected her to be, and didn't mind a bit. Today her second word was shepherd, and when she spelled it s-h-e-p-p-a-r-d, Miss McCarley just gasped and there was as much of a commotion through the room as when Fitty Smithers had his fit.

"Why, 'Lexa, I can't believe it!" Miss McCarley exclaimed.

"No'm," said 'Lexa, and took her seat, shaking with mortification, also chagrin. She knew at once what had happened. When she heard the word she had thought of Sheppard because Aunt Rhett had been The Beautiful Miss Sheppard from Edgefield before Uncle Duncan married her.

She knew that if she told this to Miss

McCarley, Miss McCarley would give her another
chance; but she didn't tell her, and felt better, ob-
scurely, for not having done it. All the same it was
embarrassing to sit there at her desk while the spelling match went on for hours and hours—only twenty-
five minutes by Miss McCarley's clock, though—and
everybody looked at her so much. In fact so embar-

rassing that she failed to notice how nice all the girls were being to her, all of them smiling and smiling every time they met her eye, until at the end of school she was electrified to have Edith Bristow, much the prettiest girl in her room, say to her, "I wisht you hadn't stayed in at recess. I had a lickrish shoestring for you." It was almost as if the girls knew it was a special day for her.

She stayed behind ten minutes to finish her "Lincoln," and when she reached home at quarter of three, the family were already at dinner, Nell in Mamma's chair at the end of the table just as she had been for three weary weeks. The boys were halfway through their soup, Pearlie was being urged to start on hers, and Lydia had already spilled hers all over her high chair and was greatly enjoying the hubbub incident to its being wiped up. Papa sat at his end of the table looking so peaceful, as always, that the bothers of the day slid off 'Lexa and when he said, "Well, daughter, how was school?" she said, "Fine, sir," and meant it.

Dinner was about the same as always, vegetable soup and lightbread and then roast (roast beef, 'Lexa knew, though Mamma never let them say anything but roast; nice people never said beef or pork or lamb) and rice and gravy and biscuits and potatoes, of course, also Irish potatoes because Papa liked them (that was excusable because he was from North Carolina) and lots of dull vegetables and poor man's corn bread instead of riz corn bread, and old lemon pie for dessert. It was not an extra-good dinner, and 'Lexa knew that on her birthday it would have been if Mamma had been there. There would have been butter beans instead of cowpeas. Still, with Papa around, nobody could feel sorry for herself.

As Papa was dutifully prodding at the lemon pie—he didn't like it any better than 'Lexa—he looked up and caught Nell's eye. He thought for a moment, then said to 'Lexa over the tumult of Davy and Pearlie and Lydia, "Well, darling, how would you like to go with me to the Farm this afternoon?"

'Lexa hesitated, thinking of twelve long-division problems, but Nell said eagerly, "Oh, Papa, she'd love it! She loves to go to the Farm."

And 'Lexa remembered tomorrow was Saturday anyhow, so she said "Yes*sir*."

Papa said, "I was thinking it might be nice for you to go along with me and go to see Rowan Powe's little girl."

Rowan Powe was Papa's overseer at Carrollton, a very smart colored man. He could read and write and knew real things too; he could make tobacco as well as make cotton, and he even had a vegetable garden. Papa was proud of him and interested in his children.

But Papa was still talking. "Rowan's little girl has a broken leg and has to stay in bed, and I thought you might like to see her and take her some pretty pictures out of the magazines or something. She must be about your age—you are about ten or twelve, aren't you, dearie?"

"Yessir," said 'Lexa, blinking her eyes and feeling glad she wore glasses that would conceal tears if they had to come.

"Well, I will be glad to have your company, and we will go pretty soon and be home at five-fifteen sharp," he said, looking at Nell, who was gazing at him most attentively.

He seemed to think for a moment, with his eyes on Nell, who made odd little motions with her hands about her shoulders; then he said, "Oh yes, I think it would please Rowan Powe's little girl if you would put on your best dress." And with another look at Nell: "Oh yes, you might wash your face and hands."

"My *party* dress?" said 'Lexa incredulously. "Or just my Sunday dress?"

"Why, I think your party dress. Yes, by all means; she will be delighted to see it. And try to get the ink off your hands. We will leave when you are ready."

It was three-thirty then. 'Lexa did quite a lot of washing, put on her party dress—she was sure Papa couldn't possibly mean the velvet with her grandmother's lace on it but she put it on anyhow since Nell hadn't said no—and then wondered what she could take Rowan Powe's little girl. Magazine pictures didn't seem like much; she looked through the last *Ladies' Home Journal* but saw nothing left in it of any value since she had cut out the Letty Lane paper dolls. She sat down on her bed and pondered.

All of a sudden she had the thought: This is my birthday and it isn't being one at all. Why don't I change it into a sort of birthday for Rowan Powe's daughter? Without giving herself time to think, she scooped up Marguerite, the doll Aunt Pearl had sent her Christmas a year ago, still good as new because she was too grand to be played with, found all her eight costumes, even the one Mamma had made with her own hands, all French knots and smocking. She put the dresses and the two hats (one had a plume) into a big box from John

134

Wanamaker New York City that had brought her winter bathrobe, laid the doll, who looked much more lovable than ever before, on top of them. There was still room left. She put in her box of Old Maid cards without much thought, and looked around the room.

Then she stopped, appalled at what she was going to do next. She knew she was going to do it even before she verified the impulse and made it irrevocable by telling herself that when you gave a *real* present you gave something you wanted yourself. She was going to take Rowan Powe's daughter her copy of *Little Women*. The best book in the world. The book she loved most in the world, the one she had read four times and knew almost by heart; she didn't think she could sleep unless it was on the table by her bed. *Little Women*—even the name made her heart beat more gently, more affectionately toward life and toward everybody. She knew she couldn't give that book away, but she knew even more surely that she was going to give it away; that giving it away was part of a pattern; that having to give it away came naturally from its being so dear to her.

She didn't stop to think all these things, just laid it in the box, put the lid on, took another

look in the mirror, at her back this time to see that
the velvet dress was buttoned right, went downstairs,
put on her school coat, said good-by to Howard who
was vigorously sweeping the front piazza and for
some reason looked much happier than he had that
morning when they talked about her birthday, and
joined Papa in the side yard where he was goading
the car into sending up great gusts of noise and
smoke.

They drove in almost silence out of town
and over the ditch-bordered roads Papa had built on
the Farm. Papa never talked when he was driving;
he considered cars so temperamental as compared to
horses that he had to keep his whole mind concen-
trated on the car in order to hypnotize it into reason-
able behavior. When they arrived at Rowan Powe's
house he said, "I'll let you go in here, dearie, while I
go talk to my men."

Then as she climbed out of the car holding the John Wanamaker box he said, "I see you
found something for the little girl?"

"Yessir," she said, "just a few things I
didn't want."

Then she hastily stepped across the board
over the ditch in front of Rowan Powe's yard so Papa
couldn't see what was happening to her face at the

thought of *Little Women*. She blinked hard and straightened her mouth at once, because the door of the little house opened and Rowan Powe's wife stood there beaming.

"I declare, it's Mr. Ca'l's little girl. Howdy, honey, you's 'Lexie, ain't you? And gittin' prettier ever' day. I declare you beginning to favor your Ma!"

'Lexa couldn't help but smile at this though she knew it was just politeness; all the colored people told you how pretty you were just as part of saying hello.

"I came to see your little girl, if I may," she said. 'Lexa rather enjoyed using manners every now and then.

"Come to see Missie? Now ain't that sump'n? Come in, honey. She be mighty proud to see you. Thishere Mr. Ca'l's little girl 'Lexie, Missie." Then to 'Lexa: "Missie's name is Miss 'Lexa for your Mamma but we calls her Missie for short. And she mighty proud to see you."

But she wasn't, for quite a few minutes, not proud nor glad nor anything but scared. 'Lexa felt shy herself, also a little stifled in the hot bedroom that was plumb filled up with a big feather bed and so decorated with crepe paper and crayon drawings of colored people and china vases and things that there was no place to rest her eyes without seeming to stare at something. But she soon saw she wasn't half so shy as Missie. So when Rowan Powe's wife (she never did know her name) went off to the kitchen after saying, "Now you talk up nice to Mr. Ca'l's little gal, Missie," thus throwing Missie into worse agonies, 'Lexa cast around for something to say to make things better. Thinking of nothing that could do that, she silently opened the John Wanamaker box, rooted down and brought out Marguerite in all her satin and frilled glory and said awk-

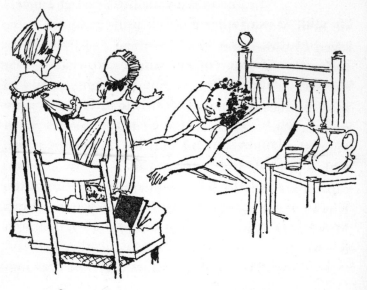

138

wardly, "I brought you a present because you broke your leg and I'm sorry."

Missie gave a snorting sort of gasp and fell back on the pillow. 'Lexa laid Marguerite across her stomach. Missie snatched up Marguerite, held her fearfully at arm's length for a moment, then clasped her to her bosom and just looked at her for about fifteen minutes, 'Lexa reckoned it was. Then she looked at 'Lexa without speaking.

"Well, I'm glad you like her," said 'Lexa, trying to give one of the little social laughs she heard when ladies came calling on her mamma.

She sat quiet for a minute watching Missie hold Marguerite, then she pulled out the other seven costumes and unfolded them one by one: the red satin, the gray taffeta, both made princess style, the yellow mull, the blue Mother Hubbard with pink piping, the flannel cape with red piping, the rose-sprigged brocade, the smocked and French-knotted challis Mamma had made, the two hats, one with a plume. Still there was silence; Missie wasn't capable of anything else, 'Lexa saw. But when Rowan Powe's wife called in, "Ain't you talking to Miss 'Lexa, Missie?" 'Lexa sprang into action—that is, chatter.

"Her name is Marguerite. And I brought

139

you something else. A book. The best book I ever read. I thought you would like to read it."

She produced *Little Women* and held it out, talking nervously so Missie wouldn't know how her very hands hated to let it go. But Missie wasn't noticing anything but Marguerite.

Finally when 'Lexa's light chatter about Jo and Meg and Amy and Beth died down, Missie said, "Is you really giving her to me?"

"I sho am," said 'Lexa, "the book too. It's even nicer than the doll."

"I thank you," said Missie solemnly.

Her mother came in just then, and her loud exclamations and miratings over Marguerite kept the little girls from having to talk. But they did talk a little, and actually got to feeling friendly when they had to conspire so hard to get in a few words to each other over the loud talking and laughing of Rowan Powe's wife.

Finally 'Lexa could no longer stand to see *Little Women* lying ignored on the counterpane. "Don't you want to look at the book?" she said. "It has beautiful pictures too."

Missie picked it up and looked with scant interest at the four New England misses disporting themselves so prissily on the frontispiece.

"It mighty nice," she said, but 'Lexa suddenly realized that far from pleasing her, the book was positively depressing Missie. The mad gleam of joy Marguerite had brought to her eyes was fading as she looked dubiously at the printed page.

"Maybe you don't like reading much?" 'Lexa suggested.

"Yes, I do—leastways I reckon I would. But I ain't never rightly learned how, not yit."

"Oh," said 'Lexa.

But her embarrassment was covered by Rowan Powe's wife's loud cackle. "Law, chile, how she going to learn to read when they start 'em learning in September when the cotton got to be picked? She haves to stay home and cook for these chillen so I can *pick*. By the time she git to school, the rest of 'em too far ahead for her to ketch up."

"Of course," said 'Lexa. Then: "Can you *cook?*" and her admiration was so real that Missie brightened at once. They had a fine time then exchanging receipts—'Lexa could make good fudge, anyhow good enough for Duncan and Wyndol. And now that they were on a congenial subject, the time flew just like when 'Lexa and Marjie were together. They both were sorry to part when Papa drove up outside, stopped the car with a great bump, and came

141

in to inquire about Missie's leg and to tell 'Lexa it was time to leave if they were going to reach home at five-fifteen sharp.

"But why five-fifteen *sharp,* Papa?" she said. Time never meant anything at home.

"I don't know, dearie," he said vaguely. "That's what they seemed to think."

'Lexa supposed "they" meant Nell; but it seemed odd.

As they started to go, she caught sight of Missie darkly gazing at *Little Women,* and all of a sudden knew what to do. "Look," she said, "I don't reckon you'd really care too much for this ole book. How 'bout me taking it back and bringing you something else? Maybe a cover for Marguerite?"

Missie literally gasped with relief and eagerly held out the volume which 'Lexa took, trying hard not to grab it.

The two girls smiled at each other as 'Lexa stood at the door, each holding her treasure to her heart, and 'Lexa feeling everything was for the best—in fact everything was wonderful.

"Oh, Papa," she burst out as they drove away, though drove is a mighty smooth word to use for their motion. "You know what?"

He didn't know the right rejoinder, so

he said, "What, daughter?" while his affectionate glance at her almost landed them in the ditch.

"I've had such a good time and she's so happy and I *meant* to give her *Little Women* and she didn't want it and I'm so happy."

"Well now, that's fine, darling, fine everything worked out so well. And your mamma will be pleased you were so generous—that was a very nice doll you gave her."

'Lexa was amazed to find Papa so observant. "Yes, if she ever gets home to *be* pleased," she murmured. Then she felt like confiding in Papa, not complaining but just confiding.

"You know what?" she began again and didn't wait for the answer. "This was my birthday and I thought what a miserable one with nobody knowing it because Mamma was away, and here it's turned out a fine one. I have Missie for a friend now, and it was fun to give her Marguerite, and I suppose it makes me feel good to think I was willing to give away *Little Women,* even though I didn't," she said reflectively.

"Yes," agreed Papa, "we can afford to feel good, anyhow a little bit, when our intentions are really good."

They drove into the side yard at home

and stopped, strangely without a bump. Then Papa, again strangely, blew the horn loudly before they got out of the car.

"You run along in, dearie. I must go up-town again," he said. "And enjoy yourself, darling," he added.

That was a queer thing for him to say, and 'Lexie puzzled over it till she reached the front steps. Then she found out the reason why. The front door burst open and about a hundred people (it seemed to her) rushed out, all singing "Happy Birthday to You," then pouncing on her, all laugh-

ing and talking and jumping up and down, at least Lydia and Davy and Pearlie were.

"Surprise, surprise!"

"Ain't you surprised?"

"You didn't guess a thing, did you?"

And there was Nell, laughing in that caressing way she sometimes had and taking off 'Lexa's coat and straightening her hair ribbon.

"Did you really think we had forgotten your birthday?" she asked, and 'Lexa knew Nell never could have.

Well, you know what parties are like, so no need to talk much about this one—just to say that if you will think of the best one you ever went to and multiply it by three, it would be about one tenth as nice as this party. All the seventeen girls in the fourth grade (and Marjie of course) were there, even Bessie Heyward who lived 'way out in the country. And they all brought presents. Eight of them brought crepe de Chine handkerchiefs, simply beautiful though not much use as handkerchiefs probably, 'Lexa thought, since if you are going to cry or have a cold you need one of Papa's big ones, but they were the stylish present to give that year and, as I say, simply beautiful, all different colors with flowers and things printed on them. And Edith Bristow brought a bottle of cologne; she wore a brand-new dress, pink with black ribbon, yards and yards it must have taken, run through the beading, the most exotic combination you could dream of. And lots of other things from the other girls. The very nicest was a blue glass vase with a fluted top and decorated with flowers; how 'Lexa liked Sarah Rogers for giving her such a grown up present.

And there was a big pile of presents from her brothers and sisters and Aunt Gabrielle and Aunt Rhett and Aunt Katy. 'Lexa didn't unwrap them now, except for the ones from Davy and Pearlie and Lyd, who all kept jumping up and down till she had opened them and she and all the girls had exhaustively admired Davy's picture of a sailboat, apparently about to capsize but beautiful, and Pearlie's pincushion which 'Lexa said couldn't have been scwed better by Aunt Rhett herself, and Lyd's present of a penny wrapped up in tissue paper that was gummy from her fond handling.

After the girls' presents had been unwrapped, admired and put up on top of the bookshelf out of reach of Lyd who was in an ecstasy of admiration and desire, Nell led the girls across the hall into the parlor. And in there were five card tables set up for Rook! Rook parties were just coming in then, and everybody loved them, grown ladies and little girls, so Nell couldn't have planned a more stylish kind of party. They played and played, and 'Lexa kept getting what Marjie said must be tenth-birthday hands, full of tens, and, more important, of fourteens too. And Sarah Rogers won the prize, which just suited 'Lexa, considering the vase.

Then, as the *Marlboro County Advocate* put in the next Thursday in its Social Notes (imagine!), "cards were laid aside and a delicious repast served by Miss Nell Carroll, assisted by Master David and Miss Pearl Carroll" (at the cost of only two plates upset, and they not on the carpet). It *was* the most delicious repast any of them had ever had at a party; Nell did have a talent for that sort of thing, as 'Lexa was always hearing Mamma's friends say. And it was the most sophisticated sort of food: patty shells with something made of chicken and, positively, mushrooms in it, canned English peas, so much more delicious than just peas out of the garden, cheese straws, and tomato aspect, as Easter called it, with olives in it (some of the girls didn't really like olives yet, but 'Lexa and Marjie did) and of course the ice cream and cake. And 'Lexa thought of the Cratchits when she saw it—there never was such a cake.

You will just have to imagine how wonderful everything was for 'Lexa as I don't know how to tell you—the presents, the Rook games, the refreshments, but most of all the feeling of being cherished by so many people. And all this glory didn't end till 'most nine o'clock. But by nine everybody was out of the house, even Bessie Heyward whose family were late getting her because they had gone to the moving-picture show—their first time, so they had had a wonderful evening too.

Nell and 'Lexa were stretched out in chairs in the sitting room and 'Lexa was just about to ask where Papa could be when they heard their own automobile horn blow jubilantly three times in the side yard.

Nell grabbed 'Lexa. "Come on," she said, and dragged her to the front yard. And there, of course, was Mamma being handed out of the car by Papa while Howard chuckled and chuckled as he toted in the bags.

'Lexa couldn't really see her in the dark, but she felt Mamma's arms around her and Mamma's stylish dotted veil pressed against her face and her heavenly smell of violets in the cold night air and her voice laughing and maybe crying a little as she said, "You see I got here! Happy birthday, darling!"

What laughing and talking there were then! The room was full of Carrolls again—somehow when Mamma was away there never seemed to be the full number of them, maybe because no one of them was all of himself with her not there. It went on and on, the laughing and talking, with even Davy and Pearlie scampering in from the nursery for a few rapturous moments with Mamma, until Mamma suddenly exclaimed, "Goodness gracious, Mr. Carroll, it's purely eleven o'clock! Everybody *run* to bed!"

As 'Lexa kissed Mamma and Papa, after saying the formal Good-night-I-love-you they all said, she added thoughtfully, "This will always be the best birthday in my life."

And so it was, till one twenty-six years later which she spent in a hospital in New York. And guess why that one was best of all?

V

Lydia Carroll Wardlaw's
tenth birthday

February 4, 1950

Lydia Carroll Wardlaw's

TENTH BIRTHDAY

February 4, 1950

IT WAS Friday night, and that is a very good night in any household. But this one was also the night before the Wardlaws' Big Day—the joint birthday of Lydia and Mother. Also it was the night when Lydia's almost-grown brother (he was in his last year at boarding school) had come home for a week end. That wasn't usually done in February, coming home for a week end, but this time their father had telegraphed the school's Head, a *very* sensible man, and said, "May we have Duncan for the week end because his sister and mother are having a birthday and his godmother is coming?" The telegram had done the work. There Dunc sat, or maybe lolled (Lydia liked just the right word always), on the poor little horsehair sofa with his legs extending half across the room, it seemed like. He was making all sorts of absurd suggestions for Lyd's party the next day while Daddy chuckled at him and Mother looked at him positively as if she were looking at her birthday cake already—gloating, that word was. Nell, Lyd's fifteen-year-old sister, had something of that look too; Lyd suddenly realized she probably had herself.

How *perfect* to have everybody home for the Birthday! And how more than perfect it would be next day when Bah would be there too—she was on her way from South Carolina right now! Bah was their Aunt Margaret, Mother's sister. She was always called Pearl when she was little and Duncan called her Bah when he was a baby, trying to say Margaret but meaning Ma, Mother insisted, since Margaret was as much of a ma to him as she was, she said. Naturally Nell and Lydia called her Bah too when they came along, and then Daddy and Mommy began to too, and now even Sophie the cook called her Miss Bah.

Think of her being there tomorrow, helping with the party, and all the girls thinking how stylish she was and how much prettier than any aunts they might chance to have, with those blue, blue eyes of hers always laughing or else looking so loving somehow, behind those eyelashes that you could hardly believe in even when you were looking at them. Lyd felt pretty sure the children wouldn't miss the television they were used to at other people's parties, with Bah here. Besides Mother had arranged a Fascinating Entertainment, she said. Mommy was inclined to be absent-minded, but if she had pulled herself together, as Daddy had urged, for this party, it would probably be simply wonderful. Mommy always knew what Lyd would like best—that was because she and Lyd were twins, having the same birthday. When Lyd was quite little, she remembered, she used to go up to Mommy at least once a day and say, "We are Friends and Twins, *aren't* we?" And Mother would say, "Ever the best of friends and twins, ever the best, Pip." Which was probably something out of a book.

Tonight Mommy was talking outrageously, egged on by Dunc, about how the party tomorrow had to end on time and how she was going to tell the mammas when they brought the children not to go away but to stay parked down on the street with their motors running for a quick getaway, when the telephone rang. It gave the rapid long peals that meant long-distance. Nell, Dunc and Lyd dashed for the back hall and the telephone. Dunc easily won with those legs, and Nell and Lyd came back to the sitting room, Nell stopping to pick up a chair that had got overturned.

"Mom!" came Dunc's yell. "It's for you. It's from Baltimore."

"Baltimore," said Mother thoughtfully as she wove her way among the piles of books on the floor.

Then they could hear her voice in the back hall raised in surprise. "Oh, Bah! Where are you? How come you are there?"

There was a pause, then the family, not pretending to do anything but listen hard, heard, "Oh, Bah, must you?"

And then again: "Oh, Bah, you'll have to wait for me. You certainly can't do anything like that without me there."

And then: "Oh, Bah, don't be silly. I wouldn't miss it for anything. I'll go figure out how to get there, and I will *be* there sometime early in the morning."

Then after another pause: "Oh, Bah, you old idiot, you know my birthday will be fun if I'm where you are, and I bet we'll both enjoy it all. But I wish I were there tonight to settle you in the hospital."

Another pause, then: "Good night, Bah,"

and then in her caressing good-night voice, just "Bah."

Her feet sounded heavy coming back to the sitting room, but she was smiling brightly.

"Well now," she announced, "never a dull moment. It seems Bah has been having a pain quite a while, and she finally went to the doctor, probably not till she was bent double though, and he said she just had to go to the Johns Hopkins Hospital in Baltimore and find out what, so she did stop off there, and they won't let her come on here, because it is an emergency and they've got to operate tomorrow."

She paused for breath or something, then

157

added, "Bah says she is all right except for having to miss the birthday and worrying for fear we will worry. But of course we won't worry. And the birthday will be wonderful anyhow—after all, Dunc is here. Maybe it would have been *too* much glory for us to have him and Bah both come," she said to Lyd, but Lyd didn't feel quite convinced.

"Now then," said Mrs. Wardlaw, putting on what she considered a brisk and efficient air, "I shall have to go down to Baltimore; I couldn't think of missing any excitement like that. But nobody will even know I've gone, I've been so clever. Everything all arranged for the party. It will go off just as well as if I were here." Then she added in a surprised and disconcerted way, "Maybe better. Nell will be in charge, just as she would even if I were here, so everything will be perfect." She beamed at Nell, who looked gravely and reassuringly back.

"Of course everything will be all right, darling," said Daddy, who was already scrambling through Mother's desk looking for timetables. "But now it's 'way past bedtime, especially for girls who are going to be ten years old tomorrow. Everybody quick to bed."

Everybody did go quickly. Having something so strange happen made you want to behave differently from usual. Lyd didn't even stay dreaming in her bath till called out, tonight.

Mr. and Mrs. Wardlaw stayed downstairs, first talking, then telephoning railroad stations and air terminals, till around midnight everything was arranged and Mrs. Wardlaw knew she would be in Baltimore well before the operation next morning.

"Now, darling, to bed!" ordered Mr. Wardlaw. "You are tired, because it is a shock to think of bad things happening to poor little Bah."

Mrs. Wardlaw batted her eyes rapidly, said in a dry tone, "Maybe so," and went up to bed. She looked in on Nell who was sleeping as usual in a way to make anybody looking at her feel somehow safe and serene; looked in on Duncan who needed another cover and was muttering in his sleep; looked in on Lydia and found her curled up in a ball and sobbing, though very quietly. The yellow hair on her cheeks was stringy with tears.

"Good gracious, what's this?" said Mrs. Wardlaw, sitting down on the bed.

"Nothing," said Lyd.

"Well, what?" said Mrs. Wardlaw. "Tell me quick, and then we'll sing."

"It's just—it's just I don't want my birthday without you." Then a great bursting sob. "We're friends and twins!"

"That's so," said Mrs. Wardlaw cheerfully, but something splashed on Lyd's hair.

She thought a moment. "I tell you what, we'll ask Daddy what to do. He always knows."

Daddy was trudging up the stairs, and came into Lyd's room now to seize her and her mother each by a hand while he listened to Mommy's explanation that they didn't really think much of spending their birthday apart from each other.

"Let me think," he said. "Of course, that's what we'll do. We'll put off the party and Lyddy-love can go with you. She will be a great help, and friends and twins can be together for a birthday in a hospital as well as anywhere else. And I can come down Sunday and fetch her home, if you have to stay."

Lyd gave a great sob of relief, and suspected that Mommy came near doing the same. Then she turned on her side and was asleep almost before her parents were out of the room.

It seemed like just a few minutes later that she was awakened by Daddy's kissing her and saying, "You have to get up now, Lyddy-lollipop, if you and Mommy are going to travel. What an adventure!"

It was indeed. To get up in the dark, dress in her Sunday coat and dress, find her seldom-worn hat and gloves, eat or pretend to eat the breakfast Daddy proudly produced when she and Mommy came downstairs, say good-by to Nell and Dunc who appeared in bathrobes and were much impressed at what was happening to Lyd, then to drive in the darkness through sleeping towns—hundreds of miles it seemed, but it took just about an hour—to the airfield. Then, maybe a little shakily, after kissing Daddy about a hundred times, to step up into an airplane, and fasten a belt around her middle. Then the awful thrill of circling around the field, then suddenly being off the earth, still waving through the window in case Daddy could see them though she couldn't see him. Then after the excitement of riding over the towers of New York City, it was all calm and almost everydayish; they took out two of the half-dozen books Daddy had put in their bag and settled down. The other people in the plane all seemed sleepy or else cross, all except the pretty young lady in uniform who brought Mother some coffee. Then Mommy fished in her pockets and brought out an all-day sucker for Lyd so they could both have refreshments. Of course, all-day suckers are never even all-hour suckers, but all the same this one lasted pretty nearly to the exciting moment when the pretty young lady came in and said, "Fasten your belts, please," and Lyd's ears began to feel funny, and Mommy said, "This is Baltimore."

It was good daylight now, probably about schooltime, but it was a dark kind of day. Still, Baltimore seemed a cheerful sort of place, es-

pecially after the bus driver answered Mother's question as to whether he went near the Johns Hopkins Hospital with "Yes, ma'am, I'll take you right there. With pleasure, ma'am."

And so he did, driving as though he liked driving, through miles and miles of streets full of red-brick houses with white steps and with lots of wagons as well as automobiles, until he came to a huge, queer-but-nice-looking building, where he turned in at the gate, drove round the circular drive-way in a very dashing manner, and let them out in front of the big front door. He took their bag from

the back of the car, took it up the steps of the hos-pital for them, collected their fare, and told them good-by as if he hated to part with them.

Hand in hand, Mother and Lyd climbed up the steps, through the heavy door and into a big hall where right in front of them there stood an enormous statue. Its bare feet were all Lyd could see at first, then she stood and gazed up and down at the figure. It was—of course it was Jesus! And there at the right of the figure, in case anyone felt maybe a little startled or confused, was a desk, and behind it a nice man seemed pleased to see her and Mommy, and when Mommy asked where was Bah (saying Miss Margaret Carroll, of course) he looked in his desk drawer and said, "Four-sixteen Marburg; I'll just send somebody to show you the way. Shall I keep your suitcase here for you?"

But Mother said no, because she had some books and her best nightgown in it for Bah, so he called a boy who picked up the suitcase and smiled at Lydia and led them through the hall and then to the left down a long, long corridor and around to an elevator. The elevator was run by a plump young colored lady with a very bright smile, and when Lyd said, "Thank you," as she got off on the fourth floor, the young lady said, "You welcome, honey."

Then there was another trip down a long hall where you could see people in bed in the rooms on either side if you were impolite enough to look, but Lyd wasn't. Then the boy stopped in front of a partly open door, and Lyd looked in while her

Mother was thanking the boy and saw Bah herself—Bah sitting there looking very white and still, but flaming into lovely joyousness when she saw Lyd's golden head peeping around the door. She stood up, and Lyd rushed into her arms. Then Mommy was there, holding Bah, and both of them laughing gently to each other. Lyd for some reason suddenly thought of Nell, and how nice it was for people to be sisters.

Then Bah said, "Happy Birthday," and asked lots of questions about Duncan and Nell and Daddy and Sophie, especially Dunc, of course. She seemed just like always. When there was a pause, and Mommy said severely, "Now what's all this?" her eyes grew bigger and darker than ever for an instant, but she said, "Oh, nothing, let's not think about the op. It will be easy with you all here. Especially with Lyddy," she said with her extra-loving smile. "And you know what?" she said to Mommy. "The nurse I have is the one who nursed old Mr. Tucker from down home when he was here twenty-five years ago!"

Then she and Mommy went off into talk about down home, especially about people and things long ago down there, and they giggled over it as much as they always had.

165

Then Bah's nurse came in and met Mother and Lyd. She was named Miss LaVerne, and she talked a great deal in a most refined way. She seemed to want to talk about old Mr. Tucker who she gave them to understand was one of her first patients (and she certainly didn't look old with all that golden hair). She remembered he had been worried about his son who, he suspected, Drank. So Bah told Miss LaVerne how the son had turned out to be a pillar of the Baptist church and a very strict father himself. So Miss LaVerne said that was gratifying—Lyd had certainly never seen a more cultured lady than Miss LaVerne; her careful tones made Mommy and Bah sound more easygoing than ever. Lyd somehow liked her better when her laugh rang out loud and natural when Mommy told her how old Mr. Tucker raised sheep on his plantation for a while and advertised in the *Marlboro County Advocate,* "Blankets made of my own wool," and everybody laughed at him, and called him Fuzzy-wuzzy, only not to his face or his family's, of course, because Mr. Tucker was a fine old gentleman.

Then Bah showed Mommy half a dozen telegrams she had got that morning from people down home who had already heard she was in the hospital—word got around awfully quickly down there, considering the South was supposed to be so slow, Lyd thought. But she guessed Bah was as special for the people down there—everybody, not just the kin—as she was for the Wardlaws. Anyhow the messages on the telegrams sounded like it.

After a while Bah felt like walking a little—she wasn't used to pain and thought the thing to do was just ignore it—so they paced down the hall to a big beautiful room next to the elevator; all glass it was, so Lyd could see out over roofs, not a very pretty sight actually, but exciting. There were other people sitting out there in big comfortable chairs. It felt more like a summer resort than a hospital, Lyd thought (not that she had ever seen a summer resort, but the heroines of some of her books had spent lots of time at them). There was a group of four ladies playing bridge in the middle of the room, two of them in negligees (one of purple velvet that made Lyd's mouth water; she loved clothes, and purple was Dunc's favorite color, so hers too, next to red of course) and two in street clothes, one in a coat that Lyd felt sure was mink though she'd never seen mink—it just had to be. The one in mink was telling the others the best place to go to have their hair done when they left the hospital, and Lyd stared and listened with the greatest interest till a chuckle at her from Bah reminded her not to.

Then when she looked at some more

people scattered about the big room, it didn't seem quite so carefree and hotelish. Especially with such an old man off in the corner, looking so waiting and with his old hands trembling so, though he held a newspaper tightly, probably to keep them from doing that. Then there were a woman and her little girl at the other end; the little girl was whining and whining at her mother and the mother's face looked as if she would normally be cross but was just too tired even for that now. Maybe this wasn't really so cheerful a place. Lyd stopped looking at people and just listened to Bah and Mommy as they talked lazily about happenings down home. But they didn't look so lazy really, kind of alert, Lyd thought.

Bah, looking down the corridor, broke off from telling about Miss Ellen Townsend's son's wife's broken leg and said, "Look down there and you'll see my doctor. No, he's just gone in somebody's room."

"I believe I'll go stand outside and buttonhole him when he comes out," said Mommy. "Then if I don't like him we won't have the operation." She rose to her feet, knocking an ash tray to the floor—Mommy and Lyd were much given to dropping things or knocking them down; they didn't mind that much though because of each other's doing it too.

Off Mommy went, and Lyd, though she was busy telling Bah how she had been going ice-skating, getting up several times to illustrate just how she fell down, was able to see her mother and the doctor shaking hands and then sitting down together on one of the benches in the hall. Mommy stayed quite a while and then came back to the sun porch looking quite pale. But she seemed very gay.

"I declare, he's lovely, Bah! I'd just as soon have an operation myself, with him."

"Maybe you need one," said Lyd. "You look kinder sick."

Bah said quickly and comfortingly, "I reckon she is hungry. It's pretty near eleven now and youall had your breakfast in the middle of the night practically."

"I certainly am," said Mommy. "And we'll soon get to eat because Bah will be going upstairs in a minute. In fact, she and I will go back to her room now, and they will get her ready. Then you can see her going past to the elevator and can wave to her. I went in her room and got your book so you won't mind waiting here awhile."

She handed Lyd *Five Little Peppers and How They Grew,* then she and Bah walked off down the hall. The bridge-playing ladies must have been listening, because the negligee one not in purple waved to Bah and said "Good luck!" And then all the others did too. And after Bah had gone, they all smiled at Lyd and one, the mink one, said, "That must be your auntie. You look like her."

So Lyd went back to her reading feeling very pleased—who wouldn't? And pretty soon she looked up at a sound of rubber wheels in the hall, and there came a colored man in white pushing a sort of bed on wheels, more of a table really, with Miss LaVerne walking proudly on one side of it and Mommy on the other. And on the table was Bah, all tightly wrapped in white things, even a white cap all over her hair, but still looking like herself because of her eyes, although they were a little drowsy. She saw Lyd standing by as they pushed the bed into the elevator, and her eyes brightened for an instant while she murmured, "Good-by, pie. I'll see you later. Eat lots of lunch."

Then Mommy's hand on her hair turned Lyd gently back into the sun parlor. "They're letting me go upstairs with Bah, just for the ride," said Mother, "but I'll be back in a minute."

Then they were gone, the elevator lumbering sadly upward. Somehow Lyd felt as if her insides were sinking as the elevator rose, but she sensibly went back to her big chair and book.

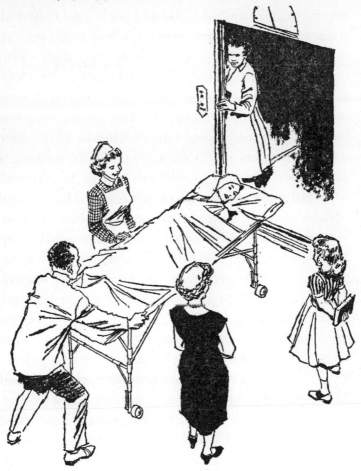

Pretty soon the sun parlor was empty except for her and the tired woman with the little girl, who was still alternately eating candy and whining.

The bridge ladies had separated with a good deal of noise, the street-dressed ones to go out to lunch, the negligee ones back to their rooms—and then something called X ray the purple-velvet one was going to afterward—and the old man had jumped up and moved out into the hall, very quickly, considering his age, when he saw a doctor beckoning to him, not a white-robed doctor this time, but Lyd could tell he was a doctor; maybe it was her romantic imagination, but she thought all the doctors in this place, anyhow the older ones, had different sorts of faces from most men; she thought the word was probably "noble."

The tired woman was talking to her child now—the first time she had found energy to do more than open her pocketbook at intervals and hand out a piece of candy—so Lyd listened.

"Marilyn, do you have to be so aggravating? If only you could be a few years older jest for this afternoon! So you could sit quiet out here and let me go sit with your granny, or else could go in her room with me and not bother her to death. Here we come all this distance and I still can't be no use to poor Ma. If only you could act like that little girl over there! Just for half an hour even."

The child paid no attention, but Lyd did, having an actual twinge (which she always pronounced twing) of sympathy as she heard the woman's long sigh of exasperation. She did not look up from her book, as she would hate to embarrass anybody by knowing about their troubles. But she thought busily as she stared at the page and came to a decision with dispatch worthy of her father.

I won't say anything now, she thought, but after Mommy and I have had lunch I will ask Mommy if I can't play with the little girl and let the lady go sit with her mother. She isn't a very nice little girl but maybe that's not her fault because maybe her mother isn't too nice either. And anyhow I know I can manage her because I can make Jean's little sister play nice, and she is certainly spoiled too.

She began making plans for dealing with the little girl whose whining, plus a developing tendency to kick, was indeed formidable, and interested herself so much in trying to figure out just what Nell would do in her case that it didn't seem too long before Mommy reappeared from the elevator and let herself wearily into a chair.

"Darling," said Mommy. She sat in silence for a moment, broken only by the whines and kicks of Marilyn at the other end of the room. Then she roused herself. "Darling, is it dreary to do nothing but wait around?"

"Of course not," said Lyd. She thought

a moment, then said indignantly, "How could it be when I've got Polly Pepper and Joel and David and Phronsie and the others with me?"

Her mother smiled in the way she always did when Lyd said just the right thing to amuse her, then rose briskly. "Let us now go have a *delicious* lunch. Baltimore cooking is wonderful, and even in hospitals, I bet. But," she added, "with you and me together, we'll probably get so lost in this big place before we find the cafeteria that we'll starve to death and they'll find our bones in some corridor years from now."

But they didn't get lost; there were so many nice people around to direct them through the long halls. When they got to the lunchroom, Mother was surprisingly unhungry after all that talk about being, and Lyd found she couldn't eat much herself; the food was all right but didn't taste like Sophie's cooking. Lyd was trying conscientiously to finish her omelet and Mommy was staring absent-mindedly at nothing, when there was a stir behind them and a gay voice in their ears.

"Why, 'Lexa Carroll, of all people—how too breath-taking! What are you doing here?"

And a large beaming lady had Mother by the hand and was talking and laughing in a way that made you feel confused, but somehow suddenly warm and comfortable. She sat down at the table with them, and Lyd soon gathered that this was Sue Thistlethwaite (Mrs. Smith now, which Lyd thought was a pity) and that she had gone to college with Mother, and, according to her manner now, had liked her very much indeed. Exuberant was the word for Mrs. Smith—no, Mrs. Thistlethwaite-Smith, Lyd decided to call her in her mind, it was so satisfying, especially if one had a tendency to lisp. And dazed was the word for Mommy at first as the floods of talk washed over her, but she soon pulled herself together to do her part in the rapid-fire conversation. After they had told each other how they hadn't changed a bit—that is, how each other hadn't; they both pointed out their own gray hairs, Mommy's not showing much in her large unfashionable coils of hair and Mrs. Thistlethwaite-Smith's admirably set off by what Granny used to call a recherché hat—they told each other about their children, Mommy restrainedly saying little about hers but looking at Lyd as if she were thinking she needn't talk; she had her evidence at hand. And Mrs. Thistlethwaite-Smith was lovely to Lyd; she beamed at her continually and patted her hand as if she were playing an accompaniment on it to her own chatter. Lyd liked this happy lady very much. She started thinking hard about what word it was just suited her, besides "exuberant," and finally, after considering several fine ones and deciding on "opulent" as the perfect one, was recalled to listening to the conversation by hearing her own name.

"But it's so dull for little Lydia to sit here all afternoon." Mrs. Thistlethwaite-Smith's rich voice rose in positive anguish, and the odd thing was you knew she felt it, anyhow some. "Now, I have such a brain wave! I am going to a matinee this afternoon and it is a perfectly nice play for Lydia to see. Oh, do say she can go with me! Then afterward we can go for tea at a perfectly super place I know. Oh, do let me have her—such fun! I'd simply adore it." She turned to Lyd. "Don't you like to go to the theater, my pet?"

Lyd's eyes darkened. Like the *theater?* There was nothing else she liked so much. She had been three times in her life, and when she even thought about it, remembering that moment when the music dies away and the curtain starts to slide up, her skin crawled with rapture. She looked at Mrs. Thistlethwaite-Smith, unable to speak for an instant.

"I see you do love it—won't we have

fun? She may go, mayn't she?" begged Mrs. Thistle-thwaite-Smith. "It is *so* dreary for a little girl in a hospital, just waiting around. And you should give *me* the pleasure in memory of old times!"

Lyd and Mommy exchanged smiles of pleasure in such graciousness. "It would be wonderful, Sue. How like you to think of it!" Mother's smile indicated to Lyd that if she hadn't especially liked Sue when they were girls together, she would from now on.

Lyd allowed herself to gloat for a moment over what the afternoon could have been, then turned to Mrs. Thistlethwaite-Smith and said, "Oh, *thank* you."

Then she went on rapidly, so as not to get shaky, "But I can't go—I just can't go."

"Oh, darling, why not?" said Mother, while Mrs. Thistlethwaite-Smith made cooing sounds of protest.

"I hafter do something in the hospital, truly I do," said Lyd, thinking of the whining little girl with more repugnance than ever. "Besides, I couldn't really leave Mommy on our birthday. Please, I can't." Her voice was unusually loud and firm, so as not to show how she was quivering inside, and her mother and Mrs. Thistlethwaite-Smith must have guessed, because they both just smiled at her and said all right darling, and all right my pet, and went on to talk about a million other things. Then Mrs. Thistlethwaite-Smith kissed them both, especially Lyd, and said in her warmest voice to Mother, "My dear, I will *pray* that all goes well!" Then in a flurry of furs she was gone.

Mother and Lyd walked hand in hand quickly back to the elevator; though they knew Bah wouldn't be down from the operating room for a while yet, they wanted to be back in the sun parlor where they felt closer to her. Lunch, even with Mrs. Thistlethwaite-Smith and all that talk—which it would probably take chapters to tell in a book, and hours to read—had lasted but twenty minutes. Maybe time goes slower in hospitals.

On their way up to the fourth floor, Lyd told her mother briefly that she wanted to play with the whining little girl so her mother could go visit *her* mother.

"Darling, are you sure?" said Mother, looking troubled but maybe a little pleased too. "I'm afraid it will be too hard for you. She doesn't seem like *such* a charming little girl."

Then they both had to giggle at such an understatement, Mom squeezed Lyd's hand harder in hers, and they stepped off the elevator, each bracing herself, Mother to face another hour of suspense, Lyd to face the whining little girl.

The whining little girl's mother looked positively as though somebody had invited *her* to the theater when she gathered from Lyd's rather shy little speech, aided by Mother's explanations, that Lyd wanted to play with her little girl so she could leave her for a while. She demurred to this plan just enough to be polite, then said, "I *will* let you help me out, then. Gee, you're a sweet kid," and went *clack-clack* on her high heels down the hall to 414, her mother's room; and Lyd was pretty sure she saw her wipe her eyes on a piece of Kleenex as she clattered along.

Mother settled down with a book, except that she would get up quite often and walk down to Bah's room and back, looking placid as always but somehow walking faster and less erectly than she generally did. Lyd settled down to play with Marilyn, and, with "Gee, you're a sweet kid" ringing in her ears, managed to keep patient and, what's more, to keep Marilyn happy. I would like to be able to say that her patience and kindness caused a change of heart in Marilyn or anyhow a change of whine, but that would not be quite true. But she was not *too* bad, and when her mother came back after an hour and a half, which did not seem any longer to Lyd than, say, the time she spent in school every day, Lyd was able to say, "I can keep her a while longer and you could take a walk or something."

But the lady said, "No, we have to catch the train home now. But I won't forget this—not ever." Then she and Marilyn went away, with Marilyn whining again, I am sorry to say.

Then Lyd and Mother were alone in the sunroom. That didn't last long; people came in and went out, mostly looking quite cheerful, but somehow there wasn't even a suggestion of hotels or summer resorts about the place now. Maybe because it was getting dark outside and Mommy kept looking at Nell's watch Nell had made her bring. Lyd supposed maybe it was making her nervous that Bah stayed upstairs so long. So she thought for a minute, then said, "If you were me, what book would you read after you finished *Five Little Peppers?*"

That did it; Mommy loved to talk about the books she read when she was little, and they talked for hours about *Sara Crewe* and *Davy and the Goblin* and *Mark Tidd* and others. Anyhow it seemed like hours; it claimed to be just twenty minutes on Nell's watch. It must really be that time

goes slow in hospitals; think how fast twenty minutes went in sports period at school.

A new and somehow worse silence fell.
Mommy pretended to be reading her book, but for-
got to turn the pages fast enough—next to Daddy,
Mommy was the fastest reader in the world probably. Lyd fell to thinking about the people in the
hospital; she wondered what the doctor told the old
man and if he were sitting somewhere else now with
his fingers still shaking in spite of himself; she wondered how the bridge-playing lady not in purple enjoyed going to something called X ray; she wondered
if the tired woman with the whining child would get
home in time to cook her husband's supper and if
he would like it; she wondered what Mommy was
thinking of and what made her so—yes, frightened.

"Mommy, do people sometimes die?" she
asked suddenly. "I mean, could they die here where
the doctors look so—so responsible?"

"I reckon so, darling," said Mother. "If
that's the way it's supposed to be."

"Is it all right? If you bring somebody
here and know the doctors here know everything, is
it still all right if they die and—and are gone, you
know?"

Then she wondered if she should have

kept still, but her mother, after thinking a minute, smiled. "I reckon so, darling," she said. "If that's how it's supposed to be."

Then she began looking absent-minded again, but at least she didn't keep looking at Nell's watch. Lyd sat still as a mouse (but couldn't laugh as usual as she remembered how, Mommy said, when she was little and Mommy told her, "Now see if you can be still as a mouse," she had replied impressively, "I'll be still as a *rat!*"). She kept willing and willing in her mind for Bah to come down again; she didn't even try to read; she just willed Bah to come down, and also she willed herself not to be frightened.

Mommy is frightened, she thought. Ever since she talked to the doctor she has been frightened. But I won't be frightened. Bah would hate me to be frightened about her, and I won't be.

So she wasn't; she just thought about the very pleasantest things she could think of, picnics in Vermont and parties down home, and most of the pleasantest things had Bah in them, so she was sitting there quietly smiling when a large white-robed figure suddenly appeared in the door.

"Mrs. Wardlaw," he said, and Mommy leaped to her feet, but overturning nothing. She looked silently at the doctor and he took her hand.

183

"It *has* been a very long time," he said. "Your sister was in grave condition."

Mommy said nothing.

"But she will live," the doctor said, with a smile that made Lyd think of the big statue on the first floor.

Mommy still said nothing; Lyd was anxiously wondering if she was going to be absent-minded with this nice doctor, when she did remember her manners, smiled just as if it were at Mrs. Van Dayn come calling, and said, "You must be tired, doctor. Do sit down."

Then the doctor and Mommy sat down and talked together, but Lyd didn't try to hear what they said. She sat off by herself and tasted relief; you can taste relief just as you could a birthday cake, she found.

Well, not much more to tell about Lyd's tenth birthday. After accompanying Mommy downstairs to telephone down home to Aunt Nell and Uncle Davy (she was almost glad Granny and Grandman weren't still living to have all this worry about Bah) and then to Daddy, she sat alone while Mommy went to stay with Bah—not really alone because people kept coming out into the sun parlor and they all talked to her, and she loved talking to people.

February 4, 1950

Mommy came out occasionally to talk for a minute, but mostly she stayed in Bah's room because Bah was coming out of the ether, and although a nurse was there—not Miss LaVerne any longer though—Mommy thought Bah might like to see a sister when she got conscious. Lyd just sat, reading some of the time, talking to people some of the time, and just thinking some of the time. And a man who came out to wait for his wife to come back from an emergency operation—and he looked as if it was a bad one, he was so quiet and gentle—talked to Lyd for a while, all about making asbestos shingles, then went away and came back with a chocolate malted milk with ice cream in it for her. What with that and also lots of chocolate from a red box a lady in a wheel chair offered her, Lyd didn't get hungry, although dinnertime came and went. But she was hungry enough to be glad when about nine o'clock Mommy came and said, "They want us to go now. And Bah is asleep now and she sent you her love. So now we can go eat a real birthday dinner somewhere."

So they did. Of course there was no place open where they could get much of a dinner, and of course there was no cake with candles, but every time Lyd thought of Bah being in such danger and being saved, she felt as if she were seeing all the candles in the world lighted at once, and she could tell Mommy felt the same.

"You know, Mommy," she said earnestly, stopping struggling for a moment with a tough piece of meat, "the girls at school would think this was a dull sort of birthday, wouldn't they? You know, so much sitting."

"They would indeed," Mommy agreed.

"Well, I don't. I think it was a *beautiful* birthday."

"Yes, darling, it was. And you can always remember that on your tenth birthday you proved you were the best friend and twin anybody could have."